WEST POINT WINGBACK

By the author of

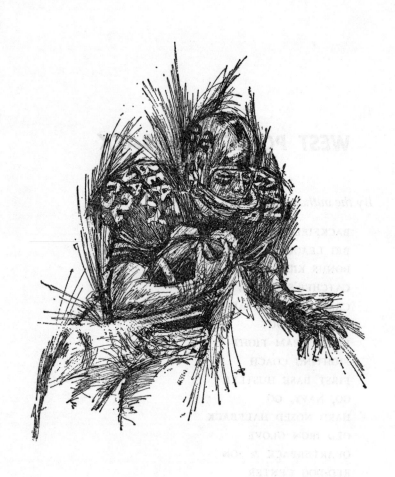

WEST POINT WINGBACK

Joe Archibald

MACRAE SMITH COMPANY
Philadelphia

WEST POINT WINGBACK

CHAPTER ONE

Syracuse, almost from the beginning of the second quarter, had pounded inside against Army, drawing in the cadets' linebackers toward the middle, their two running backs squirting through the gaps gouged out by orange-jerseyed power blocks at the tackles, mainly storming the position held down by a black-shirted cadet wearing the number 73. The bruising short gains tore out four first downs, and Army, trailing 13 to 7, was pushed back to its thirty-two-yard line.

The noise from the stands, however, could scarcely be heard beyond the west bank of the Hudson, and no great pall of gloom would settle over the academy's rugged crenelated walls that night if the game was lost, for this team on the retreat was not the big A but the lowly Army plebes, not long out of the country's high and prep schools, and the battleground not big Michie Stadium but a secondary athletic field at the Point befitting their station.

When the Army plebes took time out, Ronald Ellis Burritt, Number 73, nineteen years old, 188 pounds, doffed his tan helmet and shook grimy sweat out of his eyes. Resting on one knee gave him pain as he greedily sucked in great gobs of crisp October air. His ears ringing from the last onslaught of the Syracuse guard, he looked hopefully for respite. Joe Koch was coming in at right end, and Al "Rock" Hardison was replacing a jaded plebe in the defensive backfield. Ron lowered his head and gritted his teeth, for it seemed that Frank Troy, the plebe coach, would not be content until his right tackle was carried off on a stretcher.

At his shoulder, Steve Borek, the safety man, said between short breaths, "They're used up a little, too. They'll begin opening up," and Hardison, eager for action, slammed Ron on the shoulder in passing.

"Don't let Seller get out of the pocket. He's deadly when he scrambles."

The tackle scarcely heard him. He was gazing out toward the Hudson, at Constitution Island, at a church steeple in a little town across the river thrusting itself above the richly colored fall foliage. He felt an ache inside him that the opposition had not put there, for it reminded him of a little Pennsylvania town, and once more he felt the doubt and unease that had come from his being pressured into this austere and exacting scheme of things.

The clock began moving again and the plebes dug in, throwing their defense to the Syracuse strong side. A flanker was out for the Orange when the play unwound, and as Seller, the visitors' quarterback, retreated a few steps, Ron saw a gap in the offensive line and barreled in. Suddenly he knew he had been suckered when the Orange fullback got the ball on a draw and ran for eleven big yards before he was hauled down. The small crowd's roar of displeasure reddened his ears when he was taken out. On the side line, he was about to offer excuses but suddenly remembered they took a dim view of B-aches at West Point. He sat down next to Lew Sistak, a guard, and one of his "wives," his roommates in Central Barracks. Under his breath he said, "When I argue with that Syracuse Number Sixty-seven again I hope it'll be on the debating team."

Sistak turned a dry smile the tackle's way. "And lose the precious refuge of the training table?"

The jaw muscles in Ron's hard-boned, angular face hardened, and his dark eyes burned Sistak for a moment. He forced a grin and grunted, "Touché, Lew," and gave his attention to the action out on the field. Seller, the Syracuse quarterback, was being flushed out of the pocket. He scrambled to his right, looked for a receiver and found him covered, then ran back to the plebe thirty-four with three tacklers breathing down his neck and in his face. He squirmed loose, got a key block, and then threw to an end near the far side line on the plebe ten-yard line. The Orangeman made a great catch and got three yards before Rock Hardison nailed him. The fourth classmen in the stands made themselves heard above the shrill screams of the "Army brats," imploring the team to fight–fight–fight!

Ron got up from the bench with the other reserves and yelled encouragement to the embattled defensive line, for this could mean more than just losing a football game. The team would have to explain their ineptness fully to the upperclassmen during the supper hour in Washington Hall. Ron, as the Syracuse frosh huddled, could hear those stern and crisp voices now above the noise from the stands.

"Mister, put that orange back. I'm certain you had enough of them crammed down your throat all afternoon."

"Mister Dooflicket, you don't seem too unhappy about

9

losing. Let me see the corners of your mouth go down. Wipe that butter off your fingers."

One particularly authoritative voice seemed to wash in and over the tackle. It belonged to Second Classman Jason T. Lee, a fullback on the big Army Go-Go team. He possessed the features and the build of the typical cadet, as pictured in the public relations material turned out at the Point. He was all spit and polish, the idol of all the drags up for weekend dates, and the grapevine had it that he actually drooled when he read the skin sheets, the delinquency reports of lowerclassmen, on his company bulletin board. Ron emphatically denied to himself that his dislike for the "cow," as second classmen were called, was born of envy but chose, instead, to believe that it had to do with body chemistry. Every man in the world, it was said, made a natural enemy.

In the shadow of their goal posts, the plebes, as if they had built-in radar under their helmets, got the message and struck a brace that held the Syracuse fullback to a scant half yard. On second down, the fleet Orange right half was turned in trying to sweep Army's left flank and was racked up for no gain. Plebe noncombatants turned it on full.

"Rah!——Rah!——Ray!——Ray! U.——S.——M.——A.!"

The enemy quarterback, with less than two minutes to go to the half, kept the ball and stepped back into the pocket, but Hardison knifed his way through a pair of blockers and slammed Seller down on the fourteen. The ball squirted loose, and a plebe end covered it a split second ahead of a diving Orangeman. Here, Troy substituted only five men, one of them his first-string signal caller, Steve Borek.

Ron, content to sit it out, kept his eyes on Lew Sistak at

10

the offensive guard position, watching him trap the Syracuse tackle and let big Sid Burnett, the plebe fullback, run for nine yards. He envied the man's natural talent for the game, but even more he wished he possessed Lew's ability to take everything about West Point in stride, even the traditional "tyranny" of the upperclassmen.

"This discipline," Sistak had said weeks ago, "ha, the 'King' of the Beast Detail could learn from my old man. The flat of his hand is as big as a flounder and ten times as hard. His voice sounds like a dull power saw ripping through a hard knot in an oak stump, and what a top sergeant he would have made! When I mentioned I might not make it here at the academy, he belted me and said it had better not be because of not trying."

There had been a ring of deep admiration for his father in Sistak's voice that had puzzled Ron. He could not honestly admit that the affection he had for his own father ran to more than usual depth, even though he had been spared even a threat of the rod. . . .

Fired up, the plebes traveled like good foot soldiers, practically on their stomachs, and tore out two more first downs to their forty-seven-yard line. With little time remaining in the quarter, Borek dropped back to pass. Orangemen were stripping him of blockers when he turned the long bomb loose to Hardison, the flanker back, who caught the ball off the finger tips of the Syracuse safety man. He twisted loose from the man's high tackle and raced into the end zone, and Ron hopped up from the bench with the others to let the scoring combination hear it loud and clear. Cheers fanned out toward the Plain when Burnett kicked the thirteenth point. Army plebes, 13: Syracuse frosh, 13.

The visitors had time for only one play after the kickoff,

and the plebes had the Orange quarterback eating the ball when the time ran out. In the dressing room, the coach compared notes on the first half with his assistants before turning his attention to the players. Dan Nensinger, the trainer, passed out orange halves, and Lew Sistak bit deep into his, letting the juice squirt. "It's like feedin' a man steak out of the bull that gored him," he said, then sat down to get first aid for the ugly gash on his right leg.

The casualties, everything considered, were slight. Left end Pete "Wahoo" McGrath explored a chipped tooth as Troy called for attention. The coach singled out certain players for missing key blocks and forgetting the simplest fundamentals. He wanted to get more use out of the man-in-motion during the next half, and he made it plain he wanted this game, that would give the plebes a two-won and two-lost record for the season. Line Coach Augie Brunn took over to reveal a weakness he had spotted in the Syracuse defense.

"Their linebackers are reacting fast. They rivet their attention on our tight end and follow him when he crosses on the pass pattern. It leaves our wingback open on a trailing pattern behind McGrath."

Ron heard the coaches abstractedly. Thus far the game of football had been just an escape for him, as he swapped the discomfort of the tortured posture a plebe had to assume at the dining table for the lumps received under the tan helmet. He had long since developed the knack of appearing to be doing his very best when actually he was holding back that extra pound of effort. Next year, as a yearling, he mused, he could choose a less painful sport like track, swimming, or squash. Suddenly he felt the pressure of a pair of eyes and, looking up, saw the line coach closely studying him.

"You look mighty healthy, Burritt, considering how they clobbered you," Brunn observed. "Their Number Sixty-seven must weigh ten pounds less than you."

The plebe felt a queasy feeling in his stomach, for he thought he caught the light of suspicion in the corner of Brunn's eye. He was groping for an answer when the line coach snapped, "Don't ever give me cause to think you're dogging it, Mister. I want all that's in you—or nothing."

There was that hospital smell in the big room. It nearly always turned his stomach. Never had the contents of the textbooks bothered him, and he knew he would never hesitate to read the grades posted in every subject on every Saturday afternoon in the sally ports. The physical side and the rigors of stern discipline were something else again. Back in Grantwood, Pennsylvania, he had never had to extend himself or toe the line to any great extent, and the first day he had worked out with the plebes he felt like a kid who had been afraid of loaded guns all his life and then had been given one on his thirteenth birthday. In high school he had played football during his sophomore year and part of the next, mostly on the bench. Coaches always had their favorites.

"I'll do better, Coach," he heard himself say, above the other sounds in the room, and wondered as he spoke if he had violated the honor system. How much motivation, he would have liked to ask Brunn, does a football player have if he knows he has not a chance in the world of making the Corps eleven? Or even the B squad, that bunch of cadets the Black Knights used as guinea pigs on Daly Field every fall afternoon. They represented the opposition the Army team would meet each Saturday, and they deserved decorations for bravery. Or maybe silver discs for the holes in their heads?

13

When it was time to go out again he slowly got up off the bench, the sweat under his uniform turned cold. He took a couple of steps, then stopped, when he felt a twinge in his side. Backfield Coach Jacoby shouldered past him, saying, "Look alive, Burritt!"

Troy's basso voice boomed out, "On the double!"

Lines from the academy catalogue ran through his mind as the spectators cheered the plebes to their bench: If over a period of time the cadet appears incapable of attaining leadership standards required, his records are carefully studied by the board of senior officers of the Department of Tactics. . . . So, maintaining the required academic marks or becoming one of the greatest football players at the Point was not enough. Aptitude for the service, qualities of leadership, were even more important.

He found himself on the bench when the Syracuse frosh kicked off. George Kuska, one of the Army plebe safety men, got the ball on a short hop on the twelve, hesitated a moment to check his blocking pattern, then slammed his way up an alley that Sistak and Hardison had opened. He hit a roadblock on the twenty, reversed his field, and got eleven more yards when Cy Coker, the big center, threw a key block against a tandem of Orange tacklers.

Troy had his strongest offense in to begin the second half: Hardison, Burnett, Frohmeyer, and Borek in the backfield; guards, Lew Sistak and Keith Bellamy; Paul Ead and Tom DeGrasse at the tackles; Cy Coker over the ball; and the ends, Joe Koch and Wahoo McGrath. Borek looked the Syracuse defense over, then called a play that was a fake to Burnett. He spun around and slammed the ball against Hardison's midsection. The middle linebacker for the Orange had charged with the snap, and the faking Burnett hit him head on. Ron, on his feet, watched Hardison slant into the

14

hole off tackle opened up by Lew Sistak, who had carried the Syracuse tackle to the inside, and the right half drove for six yards before a corner defensive back hit him hard from the side.

Borek brought his team out of the huddle fast and called a variation of the previous play. Coker snapped the ball, and Borek whirled and handed off to Burnett, who was already pouring on the coal at the line of scrimmage. A crack of daylight opened between Bellamy and Ead, and the big fullback knifed through it, getting past a desperate arm tackle by a defensive Orange lineman. Burnett gave a charging middle linebacker a head-and-shoulder fake and angled for the side line. The Syracuse safety man had to cut him down on the plebe forty-nine.

Ron, although far from being a football strategist, knew that Steve would most likely call a play that could develop into a pass or a smash at the Syracuse line. He nodded his head when the quarterback called the long count to confuse the nervously shifting Syracuse defense. Borek took the ball from under Cy Coker, dropped back as if to pass, but slipped the ball to Sid Burnett. The fullback delayed for part of a second, then broke up the middle. He met a stone wall for no gain and had to be helped to his feet. When Hardison and Tom DeGrasse let go of him he immediately eased himself back on the turf, and the trainer hurriedly left the bench. Ron, his throat suddenly dry, remembered an autumn afternoon not too long ago. . . .

He had sat in a chair in the Burritt living room while his mother bathed his left ankle with cold compresses. "They piled on me," he said, just as his father came home from the hardware store. "Fraley doesn't want anybody trying to beat Eddie Lowden's time. When you're the mayor's son——"

"The ankle doesn't look swelled to me," Harvey Burritt said. "Ron, you just have to admit you went up against some real competition."

"I ought to know if I hurt or not," Ron snapped back, and appealed to his mother.

"Just forget about football," she said, "and you'll have more time for study." She turned toward the head of the household. "It was your idea that he might get an athletic scholarship, Harvey, but even if he could we still wouldn't be able to afford a regular college. When I met Senator Torrey during a political meeting just before the last election, I had quite a talk with him. We went to school together, you know. He said Ron has as much chance to get into West Point as anyone else. The cadets are not selected for their social position or their parents' money."

"Hold it, Mom," Ron had said, feeling scared. "Who says *I* want to go to the Military Academy?"

"It's either that or go to work for a couple of years before you can hope to——"

"Work at what?" Ron had asked, almost defiantly, and he remembered his father's bone-dry response.

"A good question, believe me. Your mother seems to have the only answer."

Hadn't she always? Ron asked himself, when he turned his mind back to the game. With Ted Ansell now in Burnett's spot, Steve Borek directed the attack once more. He set up the deep pass pattern after studying the Orange alignment, sending Wahoo McGrath, the spread end, and flanker-back Hardison deep into the Orange secondary. They ran routes that crossed, while Borek's blockers fought the Syracuse blitz. The plebe quarterback had to fall back to give himself time to find the deep receiver, and Ron and the others on the bench held their breaths when an enemy defensive back got by Sistak's block and slammed into the passer. Borek, just before he was hit, turned the ball loose, and it was taken by Hardison close to the side line on the visitors' eighteen, where he was immediately run out of bounds.

Syracuse called time out, and Coach Troy sent a rusty-haired guard in to replace Bellamy. Ellie Rice carried a message in to Borek. "The Orange defensive right end is committing himself to the inside on a pass rush. Go outside the man."

The stands were fully alive. When the plebe offense hopped to the line, Steve called the pattern that flanked Chuck Frohmeyer to the left, outside the Syracuse defender. He pitched out to Ansell, and Frohmeyer hit the defensive end from the outside as he crossed the line. Lew Sistak, pulling out to lead Ansell, took the corner backer out with a block that made the spectators wince, letting the ball carrier turn upfield. Ansell ripped and tore his way to the Orange six-yard line before he was nailed from behind.

Hitting a fading Syracuse line with Ansell and Hardison, Borek added six more points to the plebe total. A few moments later Cy Coker's perfect pass from center was placed down, and Frohmeyer booted it over the bar for the twentieth point.

Three plays later, with the Syracuse frosh on their twenty-eight needing seven big yards on third down, Tom De-Grasse came off, favoring his left leg. Troy picked Ron up with his eyes. "Get in there, Burritt!" He rattled off five other names as the tackle pulled on his tan helmet.

Sistak, coming in for a breather, shouted at Ron, "They're ready to fold. Hit 'em good!"

Number 73, a brassy taste in his mouth, hoped Lew was dead right when he took over with the defensive pack. He swept his eyes over the Orangemen but could not find Number 67. In his place was a much smaller guard with a spotless jersey. Time in once more, with the Orange pivot man over the ball, he matched the hostile stare of the Syracuse linemen with the best he could muster. But under his arms and knees his sweat was oozing freely.

The Orange shifted to the left, and interference swung off Ron's tackle slot. The blockers seemed ten feet tall as he set his teeth and charged. The opposing end and tackle double-teamed him, one high and one low, and his teeth got a piece of his tongue as the ground came up to meet him. When he slowly lifted himself to his feet, he wondered at the gleeful burst of sound from the seats; spitting some blood, he saw that the Orange fullback was short of a first down by three big yards. Paul Ead and Cy Coker were playfully roughing up Chuck Frohmeyer. "Where did you spring from, Chuck?" Cy yelled at the defensive back. "Yipes, what a tackle!"

The Orange had to punt. DeGrasse broke through on the kicker and blocked it, the ball bouncing free. Ron grabbed at it when it sliced off the arm of a desperate Orangeman, hugged it to his chest, and rolled over. He ground a grin against the turf and blessed a lady known as Luck. He could certainly use more of her favors at the Point.

CHAPTER TWO

The Army plebes, elated over the break, put the ball in play on the Orange twenty-two, and Sid Burnett, healthy once more, drew the Syracuse defense in tight with two line smashes that advanced the ball to the visitors' fifteen. Ron, who had teamed up with Joe Koch to take the Syracuse tackle out of the last play, smiled to himself as he joined the huddle. Troy had left him in there, a reward for snagging the loose ball, it seemed. Sure, they made the "whole man" at the academy. There was an offensive as well as a defensive in a war.

Rock Hardison took the smile off his face. "You quit before the whistle blew, Mister. You were still on your feet and could have put a block on that defensive back. Sid could have got close to a score."

"Let's see what the coach says about it, Rock," Ron said defiantly.

Steve Borek reminded them that he was running things and called for the flat pass. He shot it to Hardison, but the halfback was bounced out in a hurry on the Orange fifteen when Ron missed a block on the Syracuse end. There were still three big yards to go and only one down left to the plebes. The Orange coach sent in four rested linemen to make the stand, particularly strengthening the Syracuse midsection. Borek had his ends split and Sid Burnett in the bucking spot. The other people were employing a sliding defense, their wingbacks moving out of position to invite a play, then sliding back to meet what they hoped was coming.

Borek got the ball from under Cy Coker, faked to his fullback, faded back quickly and spotted Wahoo McGrath wide open in the end zone, and fired a bullet to the left end. Wahoo made a diving grab that brought the spectators off their seats. Plebe reserves formed their own cheering line while Burnett got ready to put his toe into the ball. The ball sailed straight and true over the crossbar, and the plebes were out in front, 27 to 13.

The Orange safety man ran Burnett's kick back thirty-two yards before he was swarmed over on his forty-seven-yard line, and here Seller, their quarterback, went for the air blitz. He got six yards with a screen, then made a first down in Army plebe territory with a down-and-out pass to his rabbit-footed left end. Ron, roughed up by two of Seller's blockers, took his time about getting up. His rib cage felt pricked with needles. Cy Coker and Chuck Froh-meyer gave him a lift and walked him around. Tom De-Grasse checked in, and Ron trotted slowly toward the bench. He heard no cheers.

A few seconds later he watched DeGrasse scramble an Orange thrust at his tackle slot, piling up the interference and flattening the Syracuse ball carrier for a yard loss. His eyes followed Lew Sistak on the next play, an attempt at the long pass by Seller, and Lew was one of the red-doggers that peeled the Orangeman of his blockers and fed him the football back at midfield. Syracuse took a time out, and the plebes turned loose a cheer for Seller as he left the game. At West Point you never jeered or hooted a vanquished foe. Sistak, replaced, glared at Troy when he reached the side line.

Not too long ago Ron had heard his father say, "I can count off nearly half a dozen men I know who reached an early grave trying for that extra dollar they never needed." It was in the tackle's mind that Sid Burnett could sacrifice a place on the big Army team trying for that extra yard in a game that rated only passing mention in the newspapers. And Sistak? Was he fearing the sting of his father's hand, or had he been imbued by the lines once expressed by General Morris Schaff, class of 1862? *The new cadet hears no voice, sees no pretentious figure, but there is communicated to him in some way, through some medium, the presence of an invisible authority, cold, inexorable, and relentless.* He remembered the first time that Lew had looked up at those words of General of the Army Douglas MacArthur, immortalized in big bronze letters over the entrance to the gymnasium: UPON THE FIELDS OF FRIENDLY STRIFE ARE SOWN THE SEEDS THAT, UPON OTHER FIELDS ON OTHER DAYS, WILL BEAR THE FRUITS OF VICTORY. The plebe had stood there for at least ten minutes, totally absorbed.

His eyes fixed on the next play but hardly seeing it evolve, Ron was aware of a faint voice he had fought to keep "off limits" since he had arrived at the Point. Subconsciously he was fearful of the truth he would have to face if it did break across the side line of his thinking.

There *were* "problem children" at the academy, the bane of Tac and cadet officers, those cadets who as yet could not be certain they belonged here, either in personality or temperament.

The tackle shook the imponderables from under his tan helmet and got up to watch the Syracuse kicker get the ball away. Willie Drumm, playing one of the safeties for the plebes, called for a fair catch on the cadet seventeen. Troy put three of his second-string backfield in, and Vince Rogowsky, the fullback, cracked over the Orange right tackle for eight yards. He seemed to have been stopped cold at the scrimmage line, but he fought his way out of the clutches of three tacklers, slid laterally, and found daylight opened up by a great block on the part of Paul Ead.

Number 73 threw a glance toward the stands back of the plebe bench. Three officers of the regular Army sat well up front, with their wives and kids—men of authority Ron wished he had known long ago. On the field, the plebes kept moving, hammering out the yards along the ground, Steve Borek calling the shots. Down the bench, second-string quarterback Elby Fitch said, "I'll never get that guy's job. How many demerits you think he's built up?"

Laughter rolled along the line, but Ron failed to chime in. He was back in that Pennsylvania town shoveling snow off the walk in front of the white clapboard house. A voice called out, "That's enough, Ron. Your dad will finish it up. Come into the house. I've made some hot coffee." He was pretty sure that was the way it had been. . . .

A sudden explosion of sound from the stands whisked voices and memories from his mind and brought him to his feet. Herbie Whitcomb, a second-string back, was knifing through the Syracuse line behind some fierce blocking. Only a block, barely missed by Cy Coker, prevented him from going all the way. Borek, a little shaken up, was taken out, and Fitch went in. On the next play Fitch rolled out of the cup when his protection was quickly stripped. He ran for it and made three yards.

Lew Sistak squirmed on the bench. Sid Burnett, with the plebes on the visitors' twenty-one, eyed the coach hopefully, but Troy stayed with the combination that was hot. The Orangemen suddenly cooled it off on the next play, their big right tackle breaking into the backfield to grab Rogowsky the moment after he'd taken the handoff from Elby Fitch. On third down, with eleven yards to go, Elby dropped back and tried to spot a receiver open, could not, and was chased back to the thirty. There he got flattened by three tacklers. Troy sent Steve Borek back in, along with Hardison, Burnett, and end Joe Koch. One more touchdown could ice it for the plebes.

Ron smelled out the fourth-down play. The plebe quarterback had Wahoo McGrath split wide to the left, and he had a flanker out. As the play unwound, Wahoo delayed, then sprinted straight ahead for several steps before faking to the outside. He left an Orange defender cross-legged when he cut sharply across toward the middle of the field. He arrived there just in time to take Borek's pass, whirled away from a tackler, and ran the last five yards to the end zone.

The try for the extra point went wide, but the partisan crowd could not have cared less. Army plebes, 33: Visitors, 13.

With only a few minutes left in the game, the Syracuse freshmen, Seller calling the signals, had to go for broke. Frohmeyer's kickoff dropped into the hands of a fast back named Canady, who was on the run when he caught it. A wedge of blockers raising havoc ahead of him, the ball carrier made it to his forty-four before being spilled from behind by a desperate plebe safety man.

In a good field position, Seller faded back on first down and threw the long bomb. It went over the receiver's head and out of bounds, but there was a flag on the play. Clipping was called against the Army plebes, and the referee picked up the red handkerchief on the plebe forty-seven and paced off fifteen yards in favor of the Orangemen. Troy went to his bench, but not in desperation. The game was his. He sent men out that needed experience, and Ron was one of them.

As he ran out, the tackle wished he had as retentive a mind regarding football as he had for the textbooks. He was digging in, his eyes on the Syracuse offensive end and halfback, before Augie Brunn's oft-repeated words of wisdom resgistered. "The inside route to the passer is the shortest, and don't depend on your middle linebacker to protect you. Fake to the outside, then break back to the inside. And always remember you don't have more than four seconds to get to that passer."

Seller dropped back into the cup and Ron went inside, but the Orange guard made the same maneuver, and on the other side of the line Paul Ead had hit inside, too. The Syracuse guards jammed them together, and Seller's bullet pass hit his man close to the side line on the plebe nineteen.

Seller, on first down, faked a pass, then handed off to his fullback. Ron, playing the edge of a split in the plebe line, was the first victim of a vicious cross charge, along with plebe guard Keith Bellamy, and the play went through for six yards. Ron wondered how fog had rolled in so swiftly from across the Hudson as he joined the defensive huddle. Willie Drumm asked him how he felt. "All right," he said, and suddenly lifted the corners of his wide mouth and won-

24

dered if he shouldn't report himself. "All right" at the Point was your word of honor. It was accepted without reservations. He knew he wasn't all right when he took his stance in the hard-pressed plebe line. He was too light in the stomach. His bitten tongue was feeling too big for his mouth.

Over on their bench, the plebes were imploring the team to hold. Seller saw another first down over Ron's slot and called on his fast halfback, Canady. The plebe got hit with what he thought were two falling timbers, and as he went down he lashed out blindly and made contact with a leather shoe. It tore loose from his fingers, and then he heard a jubilant burst of sound from the stands. He got up off the turf, feeling the hard slap of a hand on his rear. He heard Cy Coker yell, "Well, that does it!" The plebe unit crowded around him, playfully roughing him up.

"You got a piece of Canady, Ron," Willie Drumm told the tackle. "He went down like a ton of bricks and lost the ball. We've got it, pal!"

Coach Troy sent six subs in. Tom DeGrasse took over at right tackle, and for once Ron heard a few cheers as he made his way to the bench. Augie Brunn eyed him quizzically on arrival.

All right, Mister, you call it dumb luck, Ron growled inside, but maybe I've got good reflexes.

The fumble took out all the steam that was left in the Syracuse freshmen. Troy ordered ball control, and the plebes used up three minutes of the clock before they punted. The Orangemen, with Seller throwing from his thirty-one, could not go. The quarterback was eating the football on his twenty-two as the gun sounded.

The plebe squad was as happy as a bunch of nesting swallows as they peeled off in the big gym. Tomorrow they would be in Michie Stadium with the rest of the corps, cheering the big Army team that would meet invading Virginia. Ron, when he came out of the showers, had the trainer look at his swollen tongue. "Nothing but hoof and mouth disease," Lew Sistak shouted, as he reached in his locker for his gray cadet uniform. "That Syracuse guy, hoofing it, got his foot in Ron's mouth."

The coach had little to say, considering the margin of victory. There were flaws in the defense that would have to be smoothed out during the next week of practice. Augie Brunn did get a few words in close with his right tackle. "Burritt, who told you you were a stationary tackle? You haven't the weight or the savvy yet to be a retreating hand fighter. Twice, you——"

"I never realized I was doing it, Coach," Number 73 interrupted, and looked up to see Brunn walking away.

He arrived at his room with Lew Sistak twenty minutes later and found the other member of the triumvirate of Room 31 wrestling with a math book. It was a standardized room. The plain furniture was standardized, as were the amount and kind of personal possessions. The desks, chairs, and beds were alike, and so were the clothes lockers. No rugs, no pictures. Shoes shined and correctly lined up under the beds. Towels on the racks and toilet articles on the washstand laid out in the prescribed order. This uniformity of pattern, it was written, made it easy for prying Tac officers to spot any variation.

Ron involuntarily ran his eyes over the room, for this was his week as room orderly and he was responsible for anything amiss. Even a bit of dust on the underside of a lampshade, the semblance of a "rat" under a bed, meant demerits for negligence. Always, when he made this careful survey, he remembered how he used to throw his clothes helter-skelter around his room back home. His father would say, "That kid ought to clean up his room, Jen," to which his mother's stock reply was, "What are mothers for, Harvey?" Sure, didn't fathers know a kid was born to be fussed over? Well, the kids did.

"It's easy to tell who won," Cadet Leo Ralston said, as he scanned the faces of the plebe players. He was a blond youngster of eighteen years, not too stockily built and only as tall as he had to be to get into the Military Academy. His eligibility had been based on the fact that his father had lost his life in a jet in Korea. The tragedy had not scarred the plebe's sense of humor. "Dad always said he would get me into West Point if he got killed doing it," he'd told Ron and Lew his first day on the reservation.

"We clobbered 'em," Lew said. "Ron set up one touchdown for us and stopped Syracuse from making one."

"Him?" Leo asked unbelievingly.

Ron's eyes threw a spark or two. He forced a grin and hooked a thumb toward Ralston. "Listen to *him!* The only thing he'll ever dodge is a flying tennis ball. He could fall over a squash racquet."

"He's just envious." Sistak laughed.

"Maybe," the blond plebe said, holding on to his usual smile. "I just don't figure it makes sense getting your brains knocked out, knowing all the time you're going nowhere. If I'm sure I can't go all the way in anything, I don't figure to start. I'd rather be an expert parcheesi player than a third-string football player."

Ron, bothered by the plebe's inference, decided to do some studying of his own until the call to mess. He had lived long enough already with these other plebes to make accurate guesses as to what they were thinking at times, and at this moment he was positive that, if it came to pass

27

he was found wanting at the Point and shunted back into civilian life, the period of mourning in this room would be very brief.

At six-thirty the entire corps of cadets stood stiffly behind their chairs in Washington Hall, waiting for the top-ranking cadet officer's command from the balcony. "Take seats!"

Ron, at one of the training tables reserved for cadets engaged in major sports at the academy, was allowed to sit at ease, but he was not immune from the verbal jabs of the upperclassmen. His tongue, still very sore, kept getting in the way of his teeth, and a second classman gleefully reprimanded him for talking with his mouth full, although he had not as yet filled his plate. "Sir, I bit my tongue this afternoon when I was tackled. It's swelled up a little."

"As long as it doesn't affect the rest of your head, Mister."

"We congratulate you," Second Classman Jason Lee said, as he cut into a slice of cold roast beef. "After the way you handled the Syracuse freshmen, we can be sure to have a good B squad to work on another year. I'll drop around to see you," Lee added, picking up Ron with his eyes. "You must show me how you made that tackle they're still talking about—while you were flat on your back!"

The pressure finally taken off, Ron's eyes strayed toward the great mural that covered the entire south wall. Done in egg tempera, it was affectionately labeled "The Omelette" by all West Point cadets. In its broad concept it represented "the tradition of arms" and covered battles spanning twenty-five centuries. It reminded Ron of a mighty football scrimmage made up of a thousand teams, each clad in different

28

uniforms. It reflected at times the uncertainty that was in his own mind.

Not too far away, an upperclassman asked a plebe maintaining the proper brace on the edge of his chair to announce his official status at the Point. "What do plebes rank, Mister?"

"Sir, the Superintendent's dog, the Commandant's cat, the waiters in the mess hall, the Hell Cats, and all the admirals in the whole darn Navy!"

"And, Mister Dooflicket, what is the difference between a duck?"

"Sir, one of its legs are alike."

There was no laughter, no attempt at ridicule. Each plebe had his bible, *Bugle Notes,* and at times he was called upon to prove that he had studied it well. Ron, barely tasting his dessert—diced fresh fruit—remembered those days of torture, sitting straight-backed on the forward half of his chair, chin tucked well in, eyes glued to the table. He had actually dreaded the calls to mess. Plebe football had meant deliverance. A physical beating in his book was preferable to mental torture. Back home he had known neither one.

CHAPTER THREE

Autumn Saturdays at West Point when the Black Knights play at home are times never to be forgotten by Army men. The trumpets blare and the drums rumble, and the battalions march into Michie Stadium west of Lusk Reservoir, finally to form a great gray patch in the stands on Army's side of the field.

Ron, alongside Lew Sistak, after the corps had given the Virginia team a rousing welcome to the battleground, slid a soothing candy mint against his sore tongue and stared with something akin to awe at the freshly lined gridiron, much the same way as would a grammar-school pitcher look down at the diamond in New York's Yankee Stadium. If he ever heard his name cheered here it would be in his dreams.

The corps came up as one man, when Ray Sadecky's Army squad poured toward its bench, and turned loose the Rocket yell. It began with a piercing whistle, then:

BOOM!——Ah-h-h-h!
U.S.M.A. Rah! Rah!
Hoo-rah! Hoo-rah! AR—MAY! Rah!
Team! Team! Team!

"I'd give my right eye to be under one of those gold helmets," Sistak said.

"Maybe you'll have to," the plebe tackle observed.

The officials called the captains out to the field, and Army's big center, Mort Kessinger, won the toss and chose to receive. Virginia selected the goal it would defend, and then the band played the National Anthem, nearly thirty thousand spectators baring their heads to the crisp afternoon breeze.

Three minutes later, Sadecky's Go-Go team was rolling, his great quarterback, Orv Richler, using his power backs, Yale Gambrun and Jim Schaye, inside and outside. On his own forty-one, Richler threw a screen to Schaye, and the big halfback tightroped for fourteen yards along the side line for twelve more yards. Ron, after a long Army cheer, sat down and envied the skill of the Army tackle and guard on that side of the line, and hoped he could remember the moves they had made.

The Black Knights drove deep into Virginia territory, and on the invaders' nineteen, Richler, finding himself blitzed in the pocket, rolled out fast and began scrambling. He reached the Virginia twenty on his own, then picked up two blockers, and, with the entire corps up and yelling, he ripped his way to the four before he was rocked out of bounds.

Ron, as Army huddled, joined in the "Go-o-o-o, *Rabble!*"

With Gambrun in the bucking spot, Richler sneaked but was stopped a yard and a half away from the goal line.

On the next play he handed off to the big fullback, who hit inside Virginia's right tackle and plunged over with his chin nearly knocking against his knees. The racket from the corps fanned out over toward the Hudson when Schaye kicked the seventh point. Last year the Virginians had upset Army, and this first taste of revenge was sweet.

Two minutes into the second quarter, the outcome of the game was a foregone conclusion. Army had twenty points on the scoreboard, and Virginia had never been beyond the cadets' thirty. With Army moving again on its own thirty-six, Sadecky sent Second Classman Jason Lee into the game to spell Gambrun, and Ron, for a few moments, hoped that the other people would square an account or two for him when the fullback carried the ball. The "Barrow-graph" in *The Pointer* last week had said that Lee would easily be the big gun in the Army backfield during his last year at the academy. Finally he would emerge from Gambrun's big shadow.

Ron caught Sistak staring at him. He said guiltily, "Maybe it *should* happen to a worse guy, Lew."

The lines collided, making timid drags in the stands wince. The Army guard and tackle teamed to block Virginia's defensive tackle out, and Jason Lee blazed through a gaping hole and picked up seven yards.

> *On, brave old Army team,*
> *On to the fray;*
> *Fight on to victory,*
> *For that's the fearless Army way!*

Ron, his throat hoarse, turned to Lew. "I felt that Cavalier tackle get the lumps. I know just how he feels."

The game continued to be all Army. Coach Sadecky wrapped up his first line and stowed it on the bench, to wait for more rugged opposition, and let the reserves go the rest of the way.

Sancho, the smallest of the Army mascot mules, got into the next play. Hackenberg, Virginia's fastest back, was trying to swing Army's right flank. Bounced out of the playing area with no gain, he ran into Sancho before he could put on the brakes. The mule spun around and bit the Cavalier halfback on the behind before its rider could control it. For the next two minutes, laughter seemed ready to split the sides of Michie Stadium. Even the Virginia bench joined in.

The Cavalier quarterback took the Orange and Blue into the huddle, then held up a hand and called time out, unable to make his signals heard. A cadet shouted above the racket, "Sancho will be on a skin sheet tomorrow!"

Hackenberg tried to stay in, but after a running play off Army's left tackle he discovered that at the moment running was painful. The corps cheered him all the way to the Virginia bench, and an upperclassman somewhere down front cupped his hands over his mouth and roared, "We'll send you the mule's blanket, Hack!"

Army, working a punt back from their twenty-seven a few moments later, elected to control the ball for the remaining minute and a half, running routine plays into the Cavalier line. The stands began to empty.

A victory for the big team on any given fall weekend was a blessing to the lowly plebes. There would be a noticeable slack in the reins of discipline, and upperclassmen would be rather sparing of the verbal lash. Reveille was sounded by the Hell Cats, regular Army buglers, an hour later on Sunday morning, and there was nothing but chapel, relaxation, and study between breakfast and supper.

A letter from home was waiting for Ron when he returned from Washington Hall with Lew and Leo. He opened it with mixed feelings of anticipation and misgiving, for anything that pointed up the contrast between his old carefree life and the rigorously demanding new one generally shook him up worse than a head-on tackle.

"It looks like a long one," Lew said, and motioned to Leo Ralston. "We'll maybe see you later at the Fourth Class Club?"

Ron nodded, then settled back in his chair.

Dear Ron,

Now that your father has gone to his lodge meeting, I can write without interruption. Judging by your last two letters, it would appear that there might be too much regimentation at West Point, and that a lot of the restrictive measures could be ridiculous. And, as you say, it does not seem necessary to humiliate new cadets. Just keep on telling yourself how lucky you are to be there!

I am counting the days to next July, when you'll be home, and when people, especially the Bradleys, can see you in your uniform. Mrs. B. has brought her nose down to the proper level of late, and she even hinted that you might invite Sally to one of those hops you have there. How the high and mighty finally come down to earth!

We are proud of your 2.4 average in the classrooms, but we wonder why you went out for football, even though you say it is only for one year. It would seem your experience in high school would have been enough. About those boys who "couldn't take it" and left the academy—I'm sure they never belonged there in the first place.

Ron leaned back, shut his eyes, and tried to remember those days at home, filled with creature comforts and freedom of expression. He felt resentful toward the kid he used to be. His folks could have saved a lot of their sympathy; he really needed it now. This letter, as he read between the lines, seemed to remind him he was largely on his own and could no longer expect to be led by the hand. Well, they had slipped up somewhere. Take his father, now. He ran a fair-to-middling hardware business and was not what you could call an aggressive man by any stretch of the imagination, and he'd never insisted on full command in the Burritt household.

The plebe got up and walked around. Was it his fault he had been tied to apron strings too long? Perhaps if he had felt the sting of his father's leather belt. . . . He sighed deeply and read the rest of the letter. Was it wise, his mother asked, to put his criticisms of the academy in writing? Suppose, while he was called away from his room one day, he left a partly written letter on his desk and someone in authority happened to glance at it? It surely would be wiser to keep his opinions to himself.

All at once he discovered that he was feeling sorry for himself, so he hastily folded the letter and shoved it into the envelope. Oh, sure, his dad had sent his love through the proper channel. He got up, gave himself a thorough inspection, then left the room.

The Fourth Class Club, considering the demands made on its members, was never overcrowded. It was a high-ceilinged room in Central Barracks, over the west sally port, and its furnishings were a radio, a TV, a few chairs, and a small stack of magazines. A baker's dozen plebes were there when Ron arrived, taking advantage of this most welcome isolation from the Beast Detail. "You make sure the place hasn't been bugged," he said to Sistak.

"You are assuming," Leo Ralston said, with mock severity, "that some of our upperclassmen are not souls of honor. I might turn you in, Mister."

"I doubt it. It is very easy to louse up a room orderly, if you know what I mean. You're 'it' next week. So——" Ron clamped a hand against his right cheek and suddenly fled the room. He had forgotten to indicate on the absence card where he was going. Not more than a few seconds after he had compensated, a Tac officer appeared. Ron braced while the officer checked the cards. It was "All right," and the plebe was still sweating over his narrow escape until the Tac officer's steps faded out in the corridor. Even allowing for one-third of the recorded demerits traditionally forgiven for the fourth class, he already had sixty-seven "deficiencies in conduct" marked against him. One hundred and fifteen brought a cadet in front of the Academic Board and generally meant dismissal from the academy.

He was still a little shaken up when he returned to the Fourth Class Club. There he found Lew Sistak demonstrating the straight shoulder charge with Keith Bellamy as the victim. "All right, the snap," the plebe guard grunted, then drove in at Lew with short, choppy steps and hit him with his full weight. "Fists—close to—the chest—like this. Arms close to the—body. Elbows out—back straight—rump low." Cadet Bellamy went tumbling backwards, and Ron had to throw a block on him from the side to save the TV set from destruction. "You knucklehead," he yelled at Sistak, "you're football crazy!"

"It's one of the big reasons for my being here," Lew said. "All-State high school guard, remember?"

Ron nodded. "But you're sure no All-State mental giant, with a bare two-point rating with the books."

"Look, you two," Leo Ralston cut in, "knock it off or——"

"I read him loud and clear," Sistak said. "A graduate who was a football hero here gets a little more recognition at an Army base, and promotion comes faster, even if his military savvy is not exactly on a par with a Robert E. Lee's. At least I'm honest about my motives. Can you say as much, Ron?"

An uncomfortable silence gripped the room for a long moment. Then Ron walked up to Lew and grinned, placing a fist lightly against the side of the plebe's jaw. "Sorry, Lew. I'm a big mouth—it's the pressure here. Who else can I sound off against but a plebe?"

Sistak grinned and poked Ron in the ribs. "I don't remember one word we said."

"If you ask me," Joe Koch said, "the uniform got the both of you hooked."

"I hear you're on the Ring and Crest Committee, Joe," Cadet Ralston said. "If you haven't decided on the crest we're going to use, I've got a suggestion. An ox yoke resting on two crossed bull whips."

After chapel the next morning, walking toward the library along Jefferson Road, Ron and Lew passed an upperclassman squiring one of the prettiest brunettes they had ever seen. The cadet wore the insignia of a battalion operations officer on his sleeve and did not choose to even glance the plebes' way. "Yow!" Lew said under his breath, when at a safe distance. "Now I have the courage to go on. You have a drag back home?"

Ron said, shaking his head, "No special one. I used to take a couple of them home my last couple of years at high school but my m——the family didn't exactly like the idea. Who needs them when the cadet hostess has a list of dates as long as both our arms?"

"That cadet is most likely headed for Flirtation Walk," Sistak said, a ring of envy in his voice. "I always figured it was a strange place to put that white marble bench, a memorial for that cadet, Sheridan, who got it for keeps in the Yale Bowl. He went in head-on at Yale's Lassiter who had already run back a punt for a touchdown. Albie Booth was the Eli quarterback then, and——"

"Thanks for the moral support," Ron snapped. "That's one traditional landmark here I never wrote home about."

"Look, I knew a kid who fell down while playing croquet and broke both his arms, Ron. He most likely stiffened up when he fell. Like when a tackler hits you, you just go limp and so relaxed that you——"

"Let's stay off the football field until tomorrow afternoon, Lew. O.K.?"

"Sure, but our business is going to be war when we get out of the Point, and I mean maybe more than a cold one," the guard said. "The game is the closest thing to war. They say that's why a lot of foreign dignitaries visit here. You read about the ancient battles or some of the modern ones, how a right or left enemy flank was turned, and——"

"All right. I won't bet that you won't talk yourself into the Heisman trophy, even though you could spend nine-tenths of the time on Sadecky's bench."

Again he was seized by a feeling of near panic. All around him the weathered piles of rugged granite built on the high rock cliffs buttressing the Plain seemed to close in on him. They conjured up granite faces that forcibly reminded him of the fact that he would do their bidding for four long years. The urge to return to his carefree world was overpowering, one big ache that clawed at his stomach. Right now, if he were home, he would be raiding the icebox. Then he would go down to Hall's Drugstore and get himself an ice cream soda. Afterwards he would go home and look at television as long as he pleased. He would go to bed and get up in the morning when he pleased.

Lew Sistak said, as they retraced their steps, "I can tell. It's eating at you again. Oh, I get it at times, and then I think of my old man. Let *me* go over the hill, and he'd beat my brains out. Believe me, I'm safer here!"

Again Ron envied Lew Sistak.

CHAPTER FOUR

The following afternoon, a class of plebes was wrestling with algebra in Thayer Hall. Halfway through the hour, Ron's mind strayed away from Cayley and Sylvester's definition of binary forms and polynomials and became concerned with a defensive tackle's assignment when the offensive team had the ball on third down with seven yards to gain. *The play would most likely go outside, so I'd drive off the wingback, or in deep. If it looks like a pass, I hold the end in.* He was mentally pulling himself out from under a pair of opposing linemen when Major Carruther's voice straightened him in his chair. "Are you with us, Burritt?"

Leo Ralston snickered himself onto the skin sheet just before Ron was sent to the blackboard to demonstrate a variable of one or more fundamental forms according to Cayley. The instructor nodded his approval and said, "I realize, Burritt, that this is a course you take in stride, but we'd all be grateful for your full attention."

It had been that way since the first morning class, since the Hell Cats had lifted the cadets out of their beds. It was in Ron's mind now that his well-being at the Point might depend more on the good graces of the plebe coaches than it did on words of approval from the academic staff. Right now he was willing to forfeit a few points mentally to acquire more physically. . . .

Football time came around much too fast. Shortly before four, Augie Brunn put his plebe squad through skull practice in the gymnasium, and Ron wished he could absorb those chalked diagrams on the board as easily as he did algebra equations. Brunn pounded cooperative defensive fundamentals into his players.

"It's a safe bet that a good ninety per cent of quarterbacks will call the following plays. Having five yards to gain, you can look for end runs and reverses, off-tackle plays, forward or lateral passes—any play that will go outside the defensive ends. With less than five to go, look for the bucks or fake bucks—any play that will go inside the two offensive ends. On third down, when they have more than five to gain and are outside their forty-yard line, look for the pass.

"Stop the strong plays, and the weak ones will take care of themselves." Brunn's pointer stabbed at a diagram on the board. "The entire line charges toward the strength of the formation if strength is toward the left. The left defensive end goes in deep, and the rest of the linemen charge to the left, covering their assigned territories. When a player elects to 'showboat' and forgets his assigned territory, he puts more pressure on the backers-up. Here the short-side tackle diverges toward the strength, protecting the short-side guard's outside territory and insuring against short-side bucks. It's looping line play."

Brunn refreshed the plebes' minds in the art of breaking

up double-teaming and gave them an illustration of the end and tackle crisscross. A few minutes later they were on their way to the practice field.

The offensive team, after the warm-up, went through their plays smoothly, running the pass patterns at top speed. Augie Brunn's charges, on the other hand, tried his usually mild disposition, particularly Ron and end Joe Koch. Working against second- and third-stringers during a less than passive scrimmage, Ron was being taken by leg whips and blast blocks. They drew him inside to run outside his tackle spot. Koch seemed to have left all his knowledge of end play in the Syracuse game. The blockers were getting to him when he was slow coming in, or they flanked him.

"Burritt!" the line coach fairly yelled. "You have to remember there's more than the guard playing on you in an offensive line. There's a center waiting to take a shot at you, and a tackle blocking down on you. And try to read the blocks. That last time the guard gave you daylight you fell for it, and almost six yards were made through where you'd been. You're not using all the power in your initial charge. Stop loafing, Burritt!"

Ron said, under his breath, "I had no idea I was, Coach." He wondered if Brunn shouldn't take a look at the graph of a human body that hung on the wall, back at the gym, and read the sign that went along with it. GAMES ARE NOT WON ON THE RUBBING TABLE. The stuff in the trainers' glass cabinet might remind him to cut down the risk of injuries during the workouts. He set his teeth as he put his helmet back on. The teams lined up again and Harry Porter, a third-string halfback, came driving toward his slot. Ron hit the opposing end's shoulders with the flat of his hands, with weight of body and rear leg coming forward in one count, and knocked him to the left, then sliced through and

42

slammed a blocker against the ball carrier, clobbering the play.

Brunn moved in but did not give Ron a word or a glance. He called the offensive guards for pulling out of the line too late. Number 73, when the line coach called for the action to continue, felt a twinge in his right elbow. He favored it on the next play, and the offense ran over him, and this time Brunn gave him all the attention he could ask for.

With a slight edge to his voice, Ron informed the coach that he had played it with one good arm. He held that elbow tight against his side.

"All right, have the trainer look at it," Brunn said.

On the side line for the next few minutes, after Dan Nensinger had given him a preliminary check, Ron, his eyes mainly on Lew Sistak, watched the offensive team go through a signal drill and then run the key plays against a ragtag line, and he could not see, barring a serious injury, how the youngster could fail to make the corps team. Lew had all of it, Ron had to admit. The size, deception, speed, and amazing agility. There was little doubt but that Ray Sadecky had already been given a book on the plebe.

Ron assured the coaches he was all right and joined the defense in protection against passes, and for the most part he remembered his assignments and even broke into the "enemy" backfield on two occasions to feed the ball to Elby Fitch, the quarterback. Finally, Troy ordered the squad to take two laps around the field. Brunn gave Ron an extra lap, and the tackle remembered the old wheeze, "That could be for nothing, so just look out."

When he came into the dressing room and began stripping off his practice gear, Ron wondered if he imagined a sudden tapering off of the usual run of talk and kidding around, the letting off of steam that most always followed the rugged workouts. Wahoo McGrath, Texas's gift to the academy, gave Ron a broad grin along with a needle. "You got housemaid's elbow, looks like. All that dusting and polishing every day is no good for us athletes. I'm thinking of writing my congressman."

The laughter that followed stung the plebe tackle, for it did not seem to be with him but against him. It seemed to infer he was a gold-bricker and that the next few afternoons would be full of lumps. The sympathy he needed now was over two hundred miles away; it could only reach him by mail. "You're a real riot, Wahoo," he fired at the end. "You're as funny as a hanging," and he hurried to the showers to cool his temper.

Lew Sistak waited for his roommate to dress, his silence speaking more plainly than words.

"All right, so I'm not the greatest tackle ever to come to the academy," Ron said as they left the gym. "Just say what's on your mind."

"I don't think it's because you couldn't be," the guard said. "I've watched you, Ron. You start out with drive enough, but you burn out and don't follow through. You forget all about pursuit and let the other linemen finish a job you're supposed to handle. You don't put your heart into the game."

"You're qualified as a head doctor, Lew? We don't get psychology until next year."

"Forget it, Ron. And the next time you want my opinion, don't ask for it."

Not long after call to quarters that evening, Ron was requested to report to the room occupied by the upperclassmen Lee, Yorkin, and Durand. On his way he wracked his brain for the reason for the summons. He knocked lightly on the door, heart starting to pound. "Come in," a crisp voice said, and he removed his cap, placed it on the floor outside the door, then stepped inside and struck a brace. "Fourth Classman R. E. Burritt reporting, Sir!"

Cadet Jason Lee, while his roommates went about their own business, let the plebe sweat out the brace for a full two minutes. "Mister," he finally said, "you delivered the laundry here this morning?"

"Sir, that's correct."

The upperclassman picked a pair of white gloves off his bed. "The wrapping on the bundle was torn, Mister. You got a dirty fingerprint on this glove."

"I was not aware of it, Sir. I'll see that it goes to the laundry as quickly as——"

"You will wash it yourself, Mister, and have it back here before taps. Is that clear?"

"Yes, Sir."

"Dismissed!" the Army fullback said.

On the way back to his room, Ron's fist crumpled the white glove into a tight ball, wishing it was one of Cadet Lee's ears. There'll come a day, he promised himself, and entertained the idea of submitting an explanation to a Tac officer in view of having the delinquency report removed. But that was quibbling. It was the B-ache even the cadets frowned upon. A few minutes later he was busily engaged in washing Cadet Lee's white glove. He wished he had a scorpion to slip inside it.

All that week, the plebe coaches readied the squad for the game with the University of Massachusetts freshmen, concentrating mostly on the running game and polishing up the defense. The Bay Staters, undefeated, seldom gambled overhead, for they had a wealth of backs and a rock-ribbed forward wall. At the end of the fourth day, Number 73, his brain a little addled by being thumped around, his mind echoing the critical verbal barrage of the coaches and their piercing tin whistles, bemoaned the fact that he had not been born a rich man's son and sent to Princeton or Harvard to become an egghead instead of a second lieutenant.

After call to quarters he hit his Spanish, the subject that gave him the most trouble, and at "lights out" tried to review the plurals of substantives and adjectives in his mind, but instead the numbers 7-1-2-1 possessed him. Strong side-tackle plays well outside the end and charges one yard straight across the line of scrimmage. Don't let the end block you in, and, if the end and the wingback attempt to box you, fight to the outside. If you meet no resistance, drop low and drive to the inside. . . .

Another day dawned like all other days at the Point. The Hell Cats, with their fifes, drums, and bugles, sounded reveille at five-fifty. Sleepy cadets hopped out of beds and stuck their heads out of windows to check the flags that would tell them which uniform to wear. Five minutes later, the plebes given the duty of calling off the minutes sounded off. "Sir, there are three minutes to assembly. . . . Sir, there are two minutes. . . . Sir, there is just one minute. . . ."

A mist hung over the big Central Area when Ron and his two "wives," Lew and Leo, stood at attention as the companies formed. Finally, after all the cadets were present or accounted for, they were dismissed to get washed and shaved and to tidy up their quarters. At six-thirty the battalions assembled on Jefferson Road. Then breakfast.

Day after day, without variation. The rigid routine provoked resentment and belligerence and grimly invited plebes to dare to disobey. It ruffled tempers and temperaments for a reason. There had been days, especially out at Camp Buckner in July and August, when Ron had told himself he'd had his fill and would take the best way out. And then he would remember what his father had said when he'd asked his advice for the first time. "You'd better listen to your mother, son, like always. It's either West Point or the hardware store."

Ron sensed that he was going to have a bad day when he nicked himself shaving. He knocked over the milk pitcher at the breakfast table, and during his first class in Thayer Hall he failed to suppress a yawn that cost him another demerit. Leaving the classroom he felt a stiffness in a thigh muscle, and as he left the building he knew he was not going to complain to the trainer lest it be construed as an alibi in advance. Those days were long since gone when he'd heard an anxious voice say, "Where does it hurt, Ronnie?"

Troy sent Tom DeGrasse in at right tackle against the invading Massachusetts freshmen, and Number 73 felt both relief and anxiety. The Purple quarterback, after the runback of Sid Burnett's kickoff for seventeen yards to the plebe thirty-nine, proceeded to probe for the weak spots in Augie Brunn's defense. He sprung Bedino, his fullback, with a late-hitting play that got four yards between the Army plebes' guard and tackle. When practically the same play hit the other side of the home team's line, Ron watched DeGrasse wait at tackle, then get late hits from two blockers that wiped him out. Bedino bulled into the secondary and made a first down on the Purple forty-eight before Lew Sistak and Cy Coker got in on him and bounced him out in front of his bench.

Troy began to pace nervously up and down the line as

Trenck, the Purple signal caller, whipsawed and trapped his defense back to the plebe thirty-four, Bedino pile-driving and his jackrabbit halfback, Hauser, piling up gains outside. On first down, with the spectators screaming for the plebes to hold, Trenck faked to his fullback, pulled the ball away, feinted a pass to a flanker, then quickly straightened and fired a pass to a Purple-clad who had come over fast from his spread right-end position. The play gained fourteen yards, but a flag was down. The grab at a plebe face mask put the ball back on the Army forty-nine, and Trenck sent Bedino up the middle, faking craftily, then pitched out to Hauser, who was in full stride around the plebe right end. Hauser cut inside a bruising block on Willie Drumm, playing corner linebacker, twisted away from Frohmeyer at wingback, coming up, and gained back most of the ground Massachusetts had lost.

The plebes took a time out. Troy went to his bench and rattled off four names, Burritt one of them. Ron, picking up his helmet, swallowed saliva to get the dryness out of his throat. When he reached the defensive huddle, Cy Coker angrily spat out some water, bit skin off a bruised knuckle, and glared at him. "All right, let's see if we got somebody who knows how to play this game."

The Purple lined up, ready to roll again. When the Massachusetts center popped the ball back into Trenck's hand, Ron followed the opposing guard's pull to the left; before he could get back inside, Bedino, coming with the flow of the play, got the handoff from his quarterback and hit through the hole. Chuck Frohmeyer, backing up fast, grounded Bedino hard for less than a yard.

It was third down, and the plebes smelled a pass. Trenck dropped back, but the plebe line was in on him before his blockers could fully fill the cup, and he ran for his life. He cut and dodged away from three tacklers. On the thirty-one, Ron saw that he had a clear shot at him. Suddenly a boulder of concussion hit him from the blind side, and over a minute passed before he saw daylight again and heard the noise from the stands. The trainer was over him, working at his ribs with practiced fingers. He stared up at half a dozen faces partly obscured by plastic bars. Sistak was grinning. "You got hit good," the guard said. "I heard your breath jump out."

Nensinger kept probing. "This hurt?"

Ron, still glaring at Sistak, said, "Only when I laugh." When he stood up he wished he felt worse than he did, and that the trainer had at least found a cracked rib. Having your lungs emptied of air was commonplace in this game; you just were given enough time to fill them again. An incipient cheer came out of the seats when he moved into the offensive huddle. Sure, stay in there, Burritt. They can't hurt us.

"They need two yards," Ted Kuska, now in as middle linebacker for Troy, said. "They'll go for it." He called the defensive signals as the Purple quarterback leaned over his center's rear. The play quickly unwound, and the lines merged with the violent sounds of contact. Trenck handed the ball to his fullback belt-high as Bedino struck inside tackle. Ron came in fast and was quickly popped by a Massachusetts guard who came across fast. The hole that opened up was clogged in a hurry by Kuska, cutting in from the corner, and Cy Coker slid in fast to help contain the Purple fullback.

The chains were brought out and stretched, and the spectators and the plebe reserves sounded off when the referee emphatically gestured toward the visitors' goal line.

Troy made six substitutions, but Tom DeGrasse was not

49

one of them, and Ron slammed his helmet down. Wahoo McGrath, plastering some loose tape on his forearm back in place, gave him a small smile. "How many times do you have to be told they make the *whole* man at West Point, Mister Dooflicket?" he asked. "They don't make half-time generals."

"They make everything big in Texas," the tackle shot back, "even mouths."

It was first down and ten on the Black-shirts' twenty-seven. Steve Borek checked the Massachusetts defense as he crouched behind Cy Coker. He called a delayed counter, changing what he had called in the huddle, and sent Burnett outside his right tackle, but the big fullback was piled up for no gain. Borek gave Ron a sour glance when Number 73 pulled himself to his feet. The tackle was past caring. The Purple end had hit him first, and then a defensive halfback, and the double-teaming had rattled his teeth. Sistak banged him on a shoulder pad. "All right?"

"Watch *yourself*," Ron fired at the guard and put his head into the huddle.

The plebes started to move. Burnett cracked the middle for six yards. He hit inside his left tackle on a quick opener for two, and the crowd told Borek to gamble for the first down. The quarterback glanced toward Troy, but the coach just stared back at him, his arms folded across his chest. The quarterback brought his team out of the huddle fast, took the snap from Coker, and saw most of the Massachusetts strength converge toward the middle. Instead of sneaking he rolled out and pitched to Rock Hardison, and, behind solid blocking, the halfback made it to the plebe forty-two before he was shoved out of bounds.

Number 73 had tangled with close to one hundred and ninety pounds of the opposition, and his entire left side felt as if he had been grazed by an Army tank. He never realized before how soft the turf of a gridiron could be, and he intended to stay down for a while. Sid Burnett and Cy Coker came over, followed by Steve Borek. The quarterback said, "You look very comfy there," just as Tom DeGrasse reported in. Ron, making his way slowly toward the bench a few moments later, suddenly asked himself a question he was afraid to answer. Why hadn't the trainer come out to look him over? Once on the bench, he knew he was sitting scared.

CHAPTER FIVE

With the first half rapidly petering out, the white lines inside the twenty-five-yard markers had hardly been disturbed. The game had turned into a seesaw battle, loaded with frustrations on both sides born of fumbles, interceptions, and costly penalties. Ron had been left to cool on the bench while a third-string tackle, Cadet Wally Minot, helped ease DeGrasse's burden in the line. With two minutes left, Steve Borek hit Rock Hardison with a side-line pass, and strong up-front blocking took the halfback to the Purple thirty-eight, where he was shunted outside.

The Massachusetts defense spread, Borek hit inside the enemy tackle, Burnett reaching the thirty, and the plebes on the bench rose up and yelled, "Go—go—go!" Number 73's voice seemed to stick in his throat. Borek lost no time in the huddle and faded back again. Purple tacklers stripped him of protection, and he took off on his own. The crowd was in full cry for the first time when he finally ran the ball out on the enemy eleven. The clock was ticking off the precious seconds when he threw to Joe Koch, who had streaked into the end zone. The ball bounced off the end's fingers into the greedy hands of a Bay State defensive back, and a long-drawn-out groan only began to fade when the Purple put the ball in play on their twenty, with just seconds to go.

The intermission seemed hours long to Ron. Nensinger, briefing the wounded, finally came to him. "How is it?" he asked. "We'll need everybody in there the next thirty minutes."

Flinching inwardly at the inflection he was sure he had caught in the trainer's voice, Ron said, "I'm ready."

The coach finally let the quarterbacks alone and called for the attention of the entire squad. "You must be aware of the mistakes you made," he said. "If you don't make them twice, we can beat that bunch. I don't have to tell you that the team that scores first from now on is going to have a tremendous advantage."

Sistak sidled over to his roommate before the team was chased out. His lower lip was swelling. "Things can't be as bad as *you* look," he said. "You'll be back in there before you know it."

"Does Troy know it?" the tackle asked.

The plebes kicked off to the Massachusetts freshmen, and a tall lean halfback ran the ball back to his thirty-nine. After two running plays that ground out six yards, Trenck picked up a first down with a hook pass. He called two wide-running plays, to spread the plebe defense, and used his fleet halfback on the business end of a reverse to keep the Army defense from over shifting. With the ball on the plebe forty-six with three and a half yards to go for the first down, he gambled and won. He hit his right end, who had broken toward the center of the field, where he had gone into reverse, and raced for the side line. His momentum carried him out on Army's forty.

Ron, from the bench, saw a Black-shirt having difficulty getting up after the melee, and when the man rolled over he saw the number worn by Tom DeGrasse. Nensinger went out, looked the tackle over, then ordered him out. Troy met Ron's glance and nodded. Number 73 was detained for a moment on the side line by Augie Brunn. "Play on the offensive end and hold him up. It looks like they'll pass here. Hit toward the man in motion and keep to the outside."

The plebes set up a 6-2-2-1 defense when time was in once more. Trenck, however, decided on the play-action pass and sent Bedino in on a delayed buck; during the clash of the lines, the Purple guard held on Ron and worked on him with his elbows while the play went through for five yards. Ron stepped toward the referee and asked why a flag hadn't been thrown down. Cy Coker backed the tackle up, and the official impatiently waved them away. Under his breath, Cy ripped out, "He must have a brother that's a baseball ump and who is also in need of thick lenses."

Football-wise fans booed as the teams lined up. Trenck, his ends split and a flanker out, kept and ran the ball himself, and one of his guards opened a hole outside the Army left tackle that was good for the first down. Chuck Frohmeyer, running the defensive unit at the moment, made a T sign to the referee. Ron blessed the time out. He had been taking a beating and was not sure it had been altogether legal. He rinsed his mouth out with water and finally controlled his breathing. He looked toward the compact bunch of Purple-shirts, picked out their Number 63, and set his jaws hard.

The clock started moving. Trenck sent Bedino up the middle, but the fullback met solid rock there. The Purple signal caller dropped back on the next play, just as the plebe defense figured he would. Ron drove inside, felt an elbow slam against his ribs, and he tumbled toward the Massachusetts center to get popped hard again. Gasping for breath, he scrambled to his feet, picked up the tan helmet that had bounced off his head, and looked around for the Purple lineman. Swinging his helmet by the broken strap, he charged toward Massachusetts' Number 63. Chuck Frohmeyer and Cy Coker intercepted him, got their arms around him, and held on. "You rockhead!" the center yelled above the crowd's expectant roar. "Hold it down!"

Ron made another try at getting loose, then let his anger drain out. "Well, tell that ref—"

Tom DeGrasse came in to take over, and Chuck Frohmeyer said, as he turned Ron around and headed him toward the side line, "I'm afraid it'll cost you, Mister."

Ron looked around for Lew and saw the cadet shaking his head at him. Suddenly Sistak gave him his back and advanced toward the huddle. Cy Coker shouted at him, "Move it, Ron! We don't want twelve men on the field."

"A very fine display of military academy sportsmanship," Brunn said sarcastically, and then stepped aside when the plebe head coach took over.

"Go take your shower, Burritt, and make it cold. You're in enough hot water. I want to see you in my office at five-fifteen." He abruptly turned away and gave his attention to the play that brought a roar of delight from the stands. Ron took a backward look, saw Trenck back on the plebe forty eating the football, then quickened his step to get away before the excitement died and the attention turned toward his banishment.

Back in his room, Ron stared out of the window at Central Area, where he had walked off punishments often enough, and tried not to imagine what the plebe head coach had in his mind for him. He kept tugging at his sleeves and checking the hang of his trousers, for it felt at the moment as if his cadet uniform had become too big for him. He deeply regretted his lack of control on the field, but had it been right for that Massachusetts guard to make his own rules, knowing that West Point cadets were honor bound to turn the other cheek? The Army never pulled a punch in a real war. His thoughts were still as scrambled as the mural in Washington Hall when Lew Sistak came in. "We got 'em," the guard said. "Thirteen to six. Steve hit Hardison with a long bomb with only three minutes left."

Ron forced a smile. "Thank heavens! Maybe it'll cause the coach to forgive and forget."

"You really pulled a rock," Lew said, sighing deeply. "Just let him talk when you see him. Always the best rule here is listen and keep your mouth shut. Be dutifully repentant."

At the appointed hour, Ron reported to Troy in the coach's office in the gym. "Take a seat, Burritt," the coach said sharply, then reached for the telephone. He talked with his wife and his young son for fully five minutes, letting the plebe sweat it out.

Finally he hung up and turned toward his visitor with an air of impatience.

Ron blurted out, "If I may explain, Coach, first, I——"

"I doubt if you would convince me, Burritt." Troy leaned back in his chair and started firing. "That display of temper this afternoon was only the reflection of your inadequateness. That offensive guard played a little rough, but the referee finally caught up with him. A fifteen-yard penalty

56

put us in scoring position. No, your behavior today was the last straw and fully made up my mind that you should have chosen some other sport at the academy. I payed out all the rope, Burritt. You looked like fair material when we looked you over at Camp Buckner last summer; a challenge to my ability as a coach, let's say. Bluntly, I'm requesting you to turn in your uniform."

Ron swallowed hard. He felt sick inside. "Coach, just one more chance. I know I could——"

Troy shook his head. "I let Brunn talk me out of this once before. You fold under rough going, Burritt. A man fearful of getting hurt will get hurt, and possibly seriously. You've tried at times, I'll say that much for you, but only with your head, not your heart. I'm sorry, Burritt. That's all."

Outside, at the head of a stairway, still in a daze, Ron was like a man pausing at the brow of a hill, not daring to look down upon what was ahead, but looking back at the rugged uphill, winding road over which he had traveled. . . .

Under a hot July day, coatless and bareheaded, carrying a light nylon bag, he had plodded up the long hill with over a hundred other candidates for West Point toward that great pile of towering, forbidding gray walls. "Halt! Forward— march! Close in, there. Hurry it up!" The climb to the administration building where more raw appointees had assembled for reception and examination of their credentials. The hundreds of statements to the effect that none of them were or had ever been married, and as many written agreements that they would serve in the Army of the United States for eight years from this date of admission as a cadet, unless found wanting in the interim.

Ron had gone through his physical at the medical office

and been hustled over to the sally port of the West Academic building where he was assigned to Company C, First Regiment. He felt like a rubber ball being bounced around by the time he had discarded his civilian clothes. He felt worse when, after being fitted out with a complete new uniform, he had been turned over with the rest of the raw material to an especially picked group of upperclass cadets known as the "Beast Detail." Straight as ramrods, looking as if they had been poured into their gray jackets and sharply creased white trousers, their highly polished black shoes catching the rays of the sun, they looked the new crop of neophytes over as if they had never seen the likes of them before.

"Stand up straight! Pull those bellies in! All along the line. You look like a bunch of unmade beds!"

"Oh, that was funny? Wipe those silly grins off your faces. Throw them on the ground—step on them!"

"Get those heads up! Shoulders back—back more! Pull those chins in, along with your guts. Way in!"

The sweat had trickled down Ronald Ellis Burritt's face, resentment building inside him as he tried desperately to keep it from showing. The upperclassmen walked up and down, looking for faults that they always managed to find. The big upperclassman who seemed to be the "King," here, had stopped in front of Ron. "You don't look happy. Your name?"

"The name is Burritt."

"Your name is *Mister* Burritt, *Sir!* At the moment. For a long twelve months you will just be Mister Dooflicket or Mister Ducrot. Don't forget even once more to answer with a 'Sir' when you talk to an upperclassman. Got that loud and clear?"

58

"Yes—Sir."

The next stop had been the orderly room in the barracks to which he had been assigned, then the room he would share with two other raw cadets. From there to the barbershop on the double to submit to the regulation Army haircut. Then to the cadet store on the run for clothing and a bag of supplies, always under the sharp eyes of the Beast Detail, under an endless string of orders that routed the wits and defied any will to utter the slightest protest. Finally, the march to the Battle Monument, where in the presence of the corps of cadets they had taken the oath of allegiance.

From that day on, orders, orders, orders. Sweating under the seemingly endless drills, smarting under the verbal lashing of the upperclassmen, Ron had been reminded of the park back home where canines took obedience tests.

"You will cut corners everywhere you go, Mister. You'll walk a straight line and wheel sharply around the corners, your shoulders back, your chest extended, your chin pulled in."

"Keep off the grass. Salute every officer, Mister. You will not go beyond the restricted area of your duties."

Drill, drill, and more drill, then the first plebe hike that had tried both the soles and souls of the new cadets. Under a hot July sun they had marched in columns of twos along the road back of Michie Stadium, dressed in fatigues, helmet liners, and carrying rifles and full pack. Plodding along, Ron remembered a Boy Scout hike of about six years ago. He'd come home with raw blisters on his feet and a tale of woe stretched by his imagination. But it had been believed, and a certain scoutmaster had received a scathing letter from his mother.

The plebes had turned northwest and into a cross-country

59

trail and soon had come into view of a high granite wall at the top of a massive outcropping of rock. "Mister, what do you see up there?" a yearling had asked Ron.

"Sir, Fort Putnam," he answered the cadet officer. The sweat trickled down from under his helmet liner, and the straps of his pack began to bite through his fatigues. His throat was losing all its moisture as the column snaked through thick woods and out again. The trail dipped downhill, and the plebes came in sight of Delafield Pond. The order, "Compan—ee halt!" rang out when the column swung out of the post via Washington Gate. "Rest—ten minutes."

Cadet officers sifted out the plebes betraying early signs of wear. Ron, just as he snapped a canteen back in place, drew the attention of a cadet wearing the three stripes of a lieutenant. "That was a big swallow, Mister. Are you trying to get a belly-ache to poop out or do you think you're a camel? Fasten the strap of that helmet liner."

"Fall—in!"

The company had gone past the 9W cloverleaf, up another hill, and to a dirt road that kept climbing. Breaths became shorter and shorter. Ron felt as if he walked on hot coals, and his lungs hurt as he kept sucking in air. Rebellion was building up in him, and he promised himself an early return to the free and easy life he had known. Some miles away on the Hudson there was another heap of stone called Sing Sing, and he doubted if life there could be worse than this.

"Fall out—to the right! We'll have C-rations here!"

Sitting beside Leo Ralston, Ron had tried not to wolf his can of vegetable stew, the crackers and jam. Washing the food down, he found his water supply alarmingly low. "My feet," he said under his breath. "They feel like lumps of wood. How far is it back?"

"Just ask them to send a jeep." Leo grinned.

They cleaned mess kits in the lake, formed once more, and marched downgrade toward Highland Falls, the cadet officers flicking the heels of the plebes beginning to wilt under the strain with verbal whips. Ron had had to summon every last ounce of will power to keep from falling out alongside the road and telling the upperclassmen to go jump in the next lake, that they could have it, and that meant also the Superintendent's dog and the Commandant's cat. Somehow, he had dragged his weary body on to the finish.

In August the plebes had been transferred from barracks to Camp Buckner, where Tac officers and first class instructors gave them basic military training through periods of intensive drill and indoctrination that left their brains limp and put starch in muscles they had not used for years. During one overnight bivouac, Ron and Lew Sistak had compared doleful notes.

"One of the worst things," Lew had said, "is returning to the post. The yearlings, poor slobs like us last year, will be waiting for us, to dish out what they had to take. It sure is a vicious circle! Well, it hasn't been much worse than what I used to get at home."

The plebes returned from Camp Buckner the last week in August to be presented to the corps at a Brigade ceremony on the Plain. They passed in review to the "Official West Point March," and Ron, despite the martial music and the pageantry, could not keep his mind off the worst that he knew was yet to come. The minds under those "buckets," the plumed shakos of the upperclassmen, he knew full well, were already conjuring up friendish methods of making the life of the new class miserable. He felt the pressure of their scrutiny as if they had singled him out for the inquisition alone.

His fears certainly had been realized. . . .

He made his way down the stairway, out of the gym, hardly aware of each regulation step he took on the way to the barracks. The faces of Lew and Leo, back in his room, seemed almost strange to him. His own voice seemed to come from way out in the corridor. "I got the foot. I've had it with the coach."

Sistak slammed a book shut. "I kind of expected it, Ron. Well, there's intramural football. Or——"

"Oh, sure," the erstwhile tackle said. "Tennis, anyone? Or maybe volleyball?" He forced a laugh and slumped down on his bed. "Well, I can eat pie tonight. I wonder if I've forgotten how to swallow with my chin tucked in? 'How many names on Battle Monument, Mister? How many lights in Cullum Hall? Call out the days, Mister!' "

Cadet Ralston suddenly chuckled. "I'll never forget that red-headed kid, Adriance, the one that washed out a week ago. They had been riding him at the table pretty hard. They asked him for the definition of leather. 'It's what marines' necks are made of,' he told the first classman, "what your heads are made of, and the strap I'd like to wind around your neck!' "

Sistak gave Ralston a critical glance.

"And right now, somewhere, I'll bet he's the sorriest wise guy in the world."

"Lew, I wouldn't bet on that," Ron snapped.

The plebe guard paused in the task of polishing up a shoe. "Yeah. You'd better go and find out where you're sitting tonight. I'll try and bleed for you."

CHAPTER SIX

The first classman at the head of the table in Washington Hall lost no time welcoming the exile from the plebe football team. He immediately appointed him "water corporal," hoping in a loud voice that he would be much more efficient in the handling of the glass pitcher than he had been with a football.

"Mister Ducrot, in case you did not know, was a tackle, but when the opposing teams built better mousetraps they always found their way to his door. So today he tried to break one up with his helmet. He is a flyspeck on the image of sportsmanship at West Point. Isn't that so, Mister?"

"Sir, that is correct."

"Wipe yourself off! And let me see more wrinkles in your chin."

Ron found the evening meal a difficult and tasteless thing, for the seven upperclassmen at the table had built up a thirst bordering on dehydration. Between mouthfuls he filled the tumblers shoved toward him and kept "wiping himself off" at the frequent commands of the table commandant. Once he was ordered to examine the water pitcher to see if there were goldfish in it. Never had the order from the balcony— "Battalions rise!"—sounded sweeter in his ears. Only once before had the urge to get out from under the whole business been as strong as it was now. He doubted if he would ever get as far as Recognition Day.

The next few days were a nightmare. He drew three demerits, for not having his absence card properly posted, and found himself on the skin sheet for returning a book one day late to the library. He discovered that the competition between the sixteen company football teams was more intense than he imagined, but during his first workout with Company C, First Regiment, it became plain that the finer points of the game he had learned from the plebe coaches would compensate for what lack of spirit he might have had. He found himself able to move against the not too skillfully coached opposition with a minimum of risk to life and limb, and to take certain evasive action without raising even one eyebrow on the face of the cadet coach. How loud were the cheers when an intramuralist was carried off the field?

The day after he had made more than a little contribution toward the defeat of Company A, currently leading the intramural league, he felt some of the pressure slip away from him. Each of the sixteen companies at the academy took great pride in their athletic achievements, whether it be on the part of those playing on the corps teams or those striving for superiority on a smaller scale. Ron had to admit that his reprieve from the rack at the moment was mostly due to the excitement building up over the big game coming up with Duke. The Blue Devils had tied Navy two weeks before, and a win over the invaders from Durham, North

Carolina, would certainly have an adverse psychological affect on the Middies from Annapolis.

On Friday night the Hotel Thayer was filled. At game time the next afternoon, Michie Stadium seemed ready to spill over as the spectators stood and cheered the marching cadets. On these afternoons, with the band setting up the cadence, Ron and all the other plebes took on a lift in morale that lasted them well into the next week. They experienced, for a while, the feeling of belonging. In their places in the stands they could yell as loud as the upperclassmen and sit with their capes thrown back.

Four minutes after two o'clock, Blue lightning struck out of a clear sky. Duke, on its thirty, sprung a halfback through the right side of Army's line and went all the way. Ron, as the play developed, had kept his eyes on the play of Sadecky's defensive platoon, the Bandits, and had seen the Duke guard lure Army's Number 71 inside to be disposed of by the Blue Devils' big center, Metnovitch. The plebe coach must surely be here. Would he admit now that it could happen to the best of tackles?

Army's Go-Go offensive team began a drive on its nineteen, and Orv Richler, the Army's great quarterback, probed at Duke's defense with quick-hitting shots inside and outside the tackles. Gambrun could make but two yards, and Jim Schaye got exactly nothing. Richler glanced toward the side lines before sticking his head into the huddle; once out of it, and at the line, he had Gambrun in the bucking spot. The fullback was hitting toward the line at the snap, but Richler pitched out to Schaye, who put all his toe into the ball before the Duke linemen got in on him. The ball sailed over the Duke's safety man's head and took an Army bounce to the visitors' twenty-six-yard line.

This time the Bandits refused to be moved, and Duke had

to get the ball away. Richler directed a drive to midfield with the corps up and roaring, but there the march ended when, badly rushed, he threw a pass into a Blue Devil's hands. It became a battle of stubborn defenses for the rest of the quarter, the heavy-duty backs of both teams vainly trying to find enough daylight to plow through.

Sitting next to Ron, Wahoo McGrath said, "Just watching 'em, I feel the need of rubbing alcohol. I'm shifting to soccer next fall."

"After the 'Barrow-graph' in *The Pointer* said you and Lew Sistak can't help making the corps squad?"

"Let's hope Ray Sadecky didn't read it. Anyway, didn't that cadet predict Army would beat Penn State?"

They came up with the hundreds of other cadets when Duke fumbled on their forty-one two minutes into the second quarter and joined in West Point's Ripper Yell.

> *A——R——M——Y!*
> *A—R—M—Y—T—E—A—M*
> *AR-R-R-R——MAY-Y-Y-Y!*
> *Team——FIGHT!*

Richler threw on first down, hitting Schaye, who had charged straight ahead and cut across to the middle of the field. With two yards to go, Gambrun hit quickly up the middle and got far enough, but he fumbled, Duke recovering. The corps turned loose a mournful dirge and sagged to the seats. What was worse, the big Army fullback favored his right leg as he slowly made his way to the bench.

Ron smiled to himself. Was it not an established fact at West Point that only plebes fumbled on or off the fields of friendly strife? He was certain now that Cadet Captain Yale Gambrun was human, could bleed just like a fourth classman, and would have had enough for the day. Those Duke tacklers had rattled him his full length. Would he, right now, be able to tell a plebe how many gallons of water there were in Lusk Reservoir or how many lights in Cullum Hall?

He felt Wahoo's elbow in his ribs. The plebe said out of the corner of his mouth, "There's a cadet corporal not too far to your left who keeps watching you. I think your feelings are showing. You'd better start cheering a little louder."

Ron, when the Bandits came out, threw a quick look around. There was a cadet close by, wearing corporal's stripes, but he was completely absorbed in what was going on down on the field. Apparently, he told himself, Wahoo was passing his own judgment. When he got him where he wanted him, he'd let the Texan know he took enough criticism from the yearlings and cows. He joined in the rousing welcome for the Bandits, the defensive outfit, that proceeded to shove Duke back nine yards in two plays and then block the Blue Devils' attempt to get the ball away. A Black Knight lineman fell on the ball on the visitors' seventeen.

Orv Richler led the Go-Go unit from the Army bench, and when play was resumed, Yale Gambrun was in at full-back.

"That's the difference, Ron, between a man and a boy," Wahoo said.

The corps pleaded for a touchdown. The Blue Devils smelled a pass, and the Army quarterback stepped back and let the Duke defense seep in. He handed off to Gambrun on the delay, and the fullback got nearly seven yards on the draw. The tacklers had not pulled their punches on the big back, and he took his time about getting up. Richler gave him a hand and seemed to be telling him he had had enough. Gambrun shook his head, and, in front of the Army bench, Number 30, Cadet Jason Lee, removed his golden helmet

Schaye, in motion to the right, drew the Duke defense that way for a few short seconds, and Richler, after faking to the fullback, ran to his left and fired a pass diagonally across the field to his end, Garvey, who made a leaping catch just inside the line on Duke's four. Michie Stadium rocked when Gambrun cracked off Duke's right tackle on the next play and fairly dove into the end zone. For a few short seconds it seemed as if he had been stopped on the line of scrimmage, but he kept ripping and tearing with that extra effort that had made him such a distinguished cadet.

Ron, lending his vocal cords to the earsplitting corps cheer as the Army fullback trotted to the side lines, wondered how a man could reach such heights. Gambrun must have started preparing for this moment way back somewhere. He had been given the right push at the right time; he had been born for the academy and had not had it thrust upon him. There were excuses for those enjoying only average accomplishments, Ron comforted himself, as he watched Richler place the ball down for halfback Ed Brickhorn's try for the extra point. The ball cleared the scrimmage line and sailed over the crossbar, and the corps turned loose a roar that could be heard far beyond the main gate.

Sadecky blanketed Gambrun for the reminder of the game and let Cadet Jason Lee carry most of the load at fullback, and Ron, although he sincerely wanted Army to win, could barely control his satisfaction every time the Duke tackles thumped Lee hard. Next year, the football experts all agreed, Lee would be the big threat in the Army backfield. Once completely free of the shadow of Yale Gambrun, he would reach his full potential. Ron grudgingly admired the man's talents, all except the one he had for making fourth classmen feel like so many crawling creatures living under logs.

The game became a struggle for the breaks. The line play

turned fierce, and both coaches used all the depth they had. With less than four minutes to play, Richler slammed the ball against Lee's stomach as the big fullback hit up the middle. The hand-fighting Army line ripped out a hole, and Lee broke through Duke's secondary to the Blue Devils' twenty-seven-yard line. The long corps yell burst skyward. The ears of the cavorting Army mules stood straight up.

Duke took a time out and strengthened the defensive backfield.

Wahoo McGrath said in a raspy voice, when comparative quiet held for a few moments, "Richler'll try a couple of passes, then Sadecky will go to the toe. Look, Pete Travenko is already warming up."

Duke stymied Richler's first pass attempt, blitzed the Army quarterback on the next try, and drove him out of the cup. Richler scrambled to the twenty-six before he was pitchforked by three Blue Devil tacklers, and Travenko left the Army bench along with the kicking tee. The corps, over twenty-five hundred strong, stood with their shoulders thrown back, their stomachs sucked in, and Ron caught himself murmuring part of the Cadet Prayer.

The pass from center was perfect, and the brace of the Army forward wall as rugged as so many blocks of granite. Cadet Travenko stepped into the ball and kicked it high and far enough, and it sailed through the uprights for three big points for Army. The mighty roar of the corps built up, up, and up and nearly muffled the racket set up by the civilian thousands. A cannon roared. A cadet stood on his head on the back of a mule. Ron and the other plebes took advantage of these precious minutes of unrestraint.

"Navy felt that three points!" Wahoo yelled, his voice practically gone.

Army, the spectators making ready for the count-down, put the rush on the Duke quarterback with less than a minute to play. A desperate attempt at the long bomb on second down was intercepted by a Black Knight on his thirty-nine and run back to midfield. The crowd, the main bulk of it up and moving, began the count. "Nine——eight—— seven——six——five——four——"

The gun sounded, and the corps spilled out onto the grid-iron. Husky cadets picked Pete Travenko up and gave him a free ride. Gambrun was lifted up into full view of the TV cameras and taken to where a sports announcer had cor-ralled Richler. Fond parents and enchanted drags mingled with the tide of cadets flowing toward the exits. Lew Sistak caught up with Ron and Wahoo outside the stadium.

"Wasn't that something?" Lew shouted.

Ron nodded. Reaction was already having its way with him. The excitement of the 10-to-7 triumph over Duke would be worn thin by this time tomorrow, and on Monday morning the whips would crack and the reins tighten. "Call off the days, Mister! What is the cow? How are they all?" He wondered how many plebes could finish the first hectic year if there were no weekends. And what manner of beasts would upperclassmen be if there were no days of worship during which they could search their souls for a scrap or two of compassion?

"The big Rabble has a long way to go before the Navy game," Sistak said. "Before that they meet Iowa State, Pitts-burgh, and Syracuse. After a schedule like that you wonder how there's a whole bone left in the team."

"If you're wasting any tears," Wahoo said, "save them for the B squad. How they stand up under all that punish-ment week after week and still stay alive to play their own company games on Fridays beats the boodle out of me. I guess that's how the Army first finds out that cadets have the guts to show bravery beyond the call of duty."

Approaching Central Barracks, the plebes passed a cadet

strolling along between his proud parents. He wore the rank of color sergeant. The upperclassman's mother gave them a warm smile and a slight nod of her head. Ron's reaction was negative. Did she have to tug at the silver cord?

He could kick a football pretty good when he was nine years old, but one day he kicked the ground instead of the ball. It hurt his pride more than his foot, and he did not take up the game again until he got to high school. There the coach had brushed off Ron's preference for the backfield. And he already had a good kicker. He needed tackles. Hide Eddie Lowden, the mayor's son, in the line? Or Tim Cahill, the son of the president of the Grantwood bank?

Naturally, Ron had reported to Coach Troy as a tackle. Now, passing through a sally port, he smiled to himself. Why hadn't he ever been put in his proper place? Would he, when he finally graduated from the academy, find himself in the infantry and yearning for the artillery?

"You're really a sad sack right now," Lew Sistak said. "That's how I've got it over most of the other plebes: I never exactly led a sheltered life."

"Believe me, he can read minds, too, Ron," Wahoo McGrath said.

Halfway through the evening meal, the plebes were allowed to slide back in their chairs and take their chins out of their collars. There was no gloating over the defeat of Navy that afternoon by Notre Dame, for Army never wanted any other team save their own to humble the midshipmen. After call to quarters, Ron and his "wives" built up fanciful plans for the weekend. The cadet hostess could furnish them dates on the morrow for a picnic down at Bear Mountain. Maybe they could get special dispensation for a quick trip to New York City and take in a movie. Or they could go trout fishing.

"Let's throw away the opium pipes," Leo Ralston said.

71

"Tomorrow will be like all the other Sundays. Keep away from Trophy Point, the Battle Monument. Go to the museum or the library. Have fun. Study. Take a walk but keep off the grass. But have fun."

"Stop B-aching," Lew Sistak said. "The walls have ears."

They went over to the Fourth Class Club for a while and watched television. After Perry Mason there was a special commentary on the critical African situation. Ron said, "They'll be fighting amongst themselves there for a long time. Maybe we'll get mixed up in it. Maybe they'll take the two upper classes down to the Florida Everglades this next summer for jungle warfare training. Can you see Jason Lee's foot in an alligator's mouth?"

Lew's glance was loaded with disapproval. "If you ever had a funny bone, Ron, it must have been removed along with your tonsils. If I were you I'd try dissecting myself once in a while instead of the cadet officers. You'll have to give orders next year; you had better learn to take them first."

Ron, more than a little disconcerted, said, "Maybe I've got too big a mouth, Lew. But I'm glad I'm not going to be a plebe next year, for I think you'll be a tough yearling."

During the hour-long study period after the first class on Monday morning, Cadet Ronald Ellis Burritt was notified that he was to appear before the Bat Board, the disciplinarian tribunal of battalion Tacs, on Wednesday. Almost terrified, he put his books aside and reviewed his every move during the past week, but he could not remember one that warranted more than two demerits, even if the shortcomings had been noticed. He appealed to Lew. "Have you any idea what it could be?"

Sistak shook his head. "Unless, Ron, like I said the other night, the walls have ears."

CHAPTER SEVEN

"Well, Mister Burritt," the presiding officer of the Bat Board said, with a brittleness that made Ron's knees shake, "I understand that you do not sing during your early morning shower but prefer to circulate idle rumors during your ablutions. I am referring to a certain bit of gossip regarding a post officer's recent difference of opinion with a post taxi driver over the condition of his vehicle, and your saying that, as a result, the major in question could qualify for a well-known cigarette advertisement—and I quote—'We'd rather fight than switch.' Is that correct, Mister?"

"I do not deny it, Sir. Only later did I learn that the story was greatly exaggerated. At the first opportunity I shall apologize to the major, Sir."

"You will let this board advise you as to what you will do or won't do, Mister."

"Yes, Sir." He stood as stiff as a ramrod, listening to the

Board's evaluation of him as a West Point cadet. His academic standing was exemplary, his aptitude for the service was still an unknown quantity, and his motivation for coming to the academy not exactly clear. He still had time to get straightened around before that day of doom in January known as Foundation Day, when cadets who were "found" packed and went home, never to return. He would be able to think about that during three afternoons as an "Area Bird." He would march the punishment area in a military manner, at the prescribed quick time, and he would walk in silence.

When he was dismissed he felt completely dissected mentally and physically. His innermost thoughts had been extricated from his brain and laid out in front of all members of the Bat Board to be thoroughly analyzed. All that for the heinous crime of circulating gossip. He wondered who could have turned him in. It had to be a cadet officer of the guard, but he could not recall having seen an upperclassman in the vicinity of the latrine and shower room that morning. The walls *must* have ears.

The next few days had the quality of a ceaseless pounding. With his ordinarily rugged schedule jammed up by the punishment tours, his brain at the end of every long day felt like a chunk of dried-up walnut meat between his ears. Classes, drill, the gym, and intramural football, combined with the concentration necessary to avoid the skin sheets, stripped him of whatever admiration he'd felt for the uniform he wore. A deep longing for the peaceful Pennsylvania countryside plagued him. . . .

The big Rabble beat Iowa State, 17 to 0. It was beaten by Pittsburgh in New York's Yankee Stadium the following Saturday, 20 to 16. Ron watched the play on television, along with a capacity crowd, in the Fourth Class Club. With only a little over two minutes to go, Army appeared to have the game on ice but, electing to control the ball after putting a Pitt punt in play on their twenty-six, lost it on a fumble. The Panther quarterback lost no time throwing. He hit his man on the second attempt for the touchdown.

"They should have kicked on third down," Ron raved, banging his fist against the top of the set. "But that's Sadecky! Get a lead, then hold on to the ball until——"

"You tell him when he gets back," Lew Sistak said testily. "*You* feel bad? How about that poor halfback, Scott?"

"Pitt really hit him," Wahoo McGrath said dolefully. "I doubt if he could have held on to an aspirin tablet. Joe Scott? It'll be us pour souls that will suffer all next week. We'll have to walk on tippy-toe and maybe breathe only now and then."

"Well, what are we wasting time here for?" a plebe shouted. "You forget we enjoy first-class privileges until the team gets back? Throw back your capes, boys, and let's live a little. Anybody hungry? Let's get a snack at the Boodler's even if we aren't. The cats are away, so let's forget for a few hours that we're mice, not men."

On Monday the pressure was on again. Returning from his first class, Ron found a letter on his study desk. The handwriting on the light blue envelope was feminine but unfamiliar. His nostrils flared a little as he caught the scent of lavender. Lew Sistak looked up from a math book and grinned. "And we thought you were antisocial."

Ron turned the letter over. The return address turned his mouth up at one corner: Sarah Bradley, 56 Linden Drive,

Grantwood, Pennsylvania. Well, this was one for the books, he thought. He had enjoyed little more than a nodding acquaintance with the girl for the past couple of years.

"Come on, open it," Sistak said impatiently. "Or are you afraid your past has caught up with you?"

"Shut up," the plebe snapped, and ripped the letter open. Miss Bradley began her letter by asking the cadet not to judge her as being bold. His mother had spoken to her once or twice and had inferred that the morale of West Point plebes depended upon letters from their home towns, especially from the distaff side.

"I know we never got to know each other very well," the girl wrote, "but high school kids generally form cliques and are foolishly unaware of the fact that other nice people are around. If a letter helps once in a while——"

The second page was filled with what the younger set in Grantwood were doing for kicks, and he couldn't have cared less. The last paragraph was indeed flattering.

"Now we know for sure that the service academies do pick the cream of the crop. I hope you don't mind, but your mother gave me a picture of you she took just before you left for West Point. I know cadets have a busy schedule, but I would love to hear from you, Ron. Sincerely, Sally."

"I didn't hear any abnormal heartbeat," Lew said.

"You're darned right. 'How are they all? They're all fickle, Sir.' That's one answer in the plebe bible that makes a lot of sense." Ron sat down and reached for the books.

A half hour later he leaned back in his chair and asked himself what was so bad about this deal his mother seemed to be working on. The Bradleys set the pattern of society back home, so why not take advantage of the uniform? Sally Bradley was just about the prettiest sight in Grantwood,

76

and her presence at the June hop would have the eyes of the cadet captains popping and green with envy. That was something he could not wait to see.

"Call off the days, Mister!" the table commandant ordered at the evening meal.

Ron rattled them off. "Sir, there are nineteen days to the game with Navy. Fifty-one days to the Christmas holidays."

Although the big Army team had yet to get by Syracuse, the signs of mid-November fever were beginning to show in the eyes of the corps. Down in Crabtown the Navy team's slogan was "Make It Four!" Rumor had it they would have it printed on their helmets come that day of strife in Philadelphia. Already signs were in evidence all over West Point. BEAT NAVY! STOP BALLINGER! It was a safe bet that not one single plebe could *not* count off the days, for they would travel to the scene of battle with the rest of the corps.

On Friday, Companies C and M of the First Battalion tangled in the intramural league, and Ron, tearing into M Company's backfield, snagged a pitch-out that bounced off a back's fingers and took off for the opponents' goal line, sixty-six yards away. A yearling safety, a track man, was still far from his heels when he ran into the end zone. C Company's coach, a second classman, brought him out for a breather and eyed him askance.

"I still don't believe it, Mister. Did a bee sting you in the behind?"

"I guess it was getting my hands on the football. A lineman doesn't often get a chance."

"Ever go out for track?"

Ron nodded. There was that day he ran against Eddie Lowden and another kid. He'd come in second. "Sir, I went out for track in high school, but my folks said sprinting was too much of a strain on the heart. I—well, I had to quit."

"After watching you the last couple of weeks, Mister, I doubt if you gave them much of an argument. You only do what is required of you—but the Army expects more. Or haven't you learned your *Bugle Notes* thoroughly? Well, we've got over three more years at the Point to make up for what you weren't taught the last eighteen. Frankly, I doubt if you'll make it."

Tight lipped, Ron went to the bench and watched Company M come roaring back, in just six plays, for the touchdown that put them in the lead again and washed out his chance of becoming even a minor hero. When he went back into the tussle with ten minutes left to play, the opposing quarterback went pass crazy. It pleased him beyond words; the satisfaction of moving in on the yearling and getting just a small piece of him compensated for the lumps received. He got in a "cheap shot" at the passer, with only a few minutes left, but his team captain turned the heat on him, asking him if he had learned sportsmanship in a back alley. "You need some special treatment, Mister!"

Ron got it on the next play. There did not seem to be anybody but himself in the defensive line when the play flowed his way. He got hit from the left and from the right, and his eyes were knocked off center. When he got up he had to brace his feet wide apart to keep from falling again, until the immediate surroundings stopped spinning. He felt a little sick to his stomach, and not too proud of himself. Later in the gym, after washing off, he sought out the cadet coach. "I asked for it, Sir. I got what was coming to me."

Company M's signal caller overheard and came over. Accepting the plebe's apology, he grinned. "There's hope for you, Burritt. You weren't just taking a shot at me, you know, but at all upperclassmen—and playing your own game, not your company's. With that attitude they wouldn't even let you play on the B squad."

Ron, pulling on a polished black shoe, laid a small grin on the hard floor. *I have news for you, Mister. I won't even look at a football after this year. It'll be volleyball, swimming, or squash.* He mulled over the remark the cadet coach had made on the field, the inference that something had been left out of his formative years. Strangely enough, an inner voice suggested he ask Lew Sistak about that. He shook it out of his mind even before he left the gym.

The Orangemen of Syracuse rolled in the next afternoon, to finally depart stinging under a 31-to-19 defeat, and then all guns were pointed toward Annapolis two weeks hence. On Monday the placards blossomed. BEAT NAVY! It was chalked on the blackboards in Thayer Hall. It was the order everywhere. The respective season's records of the two service academies meant nothing. They could be thrown out of the windows and into the Severn or the Hudson. Day after day the big Rabble practiced, screened from prying eyes. Even the most difficult of the plebes watched every step and became a paragon of virtue lest a "slug" of serious proportions prevent his taking the trip to Philadelphia with the corps.

The fever approached its crisis on the eve of November fourteenth in Washington Hall. Massed cheers for the team seemed to shake the roof and bring some of the immortals on the big mural alive. Twenty-seven hundred cadets stood, spines as straight as ramrods, and sang the spirited Army songs. They paid full-lunged tribute to the big guns they hoped would sink the Navy: Gambrun, Richler, Schaye, Donnmyer, Lee, Kessinger, and half a dozen others. They thunderously saluted Ray Sadecky and his staff. We can and we will! Fight! Fight! Fight!

For the first time since donning the uniform, Ron felt it closer to his skin. They said you felt it *under* your skin, as the years rolled by, and that if you did not then the best thing to do was resign. In the barracks later, the temperature of his enthusiasm began to lessen to some degree, but Lew Sistak was still at fever pitch. "We get off the reservation for the first time," he reminded his roommates. "We'll live like the other half of the world for twenty-four hours— and at ease. A room at a swank hotel, with no beds to make or floor to sweep." He punched a hole in his pillow with a big fist. "And that's how we'll sink Navy!"

Leo Ralston said, "Man, it's about time we chased that goat. It has chewed up Army blankets for three long years!"

At Municipal Stadium, in the City of Brotherly Love the next afternoon, the corps screamed vainly for the big Rabble to overcome a 14-to-0 deficit at the beginning of the second half. Richler, using his pitching arm, along with the sheer power of Gambrun, Lee, and Schaye, drove seventy-two yards to a score to narrow the gap by one touchdown. Navy's Heisman trophy winner, Tod Ballinger, however, bounced back with a passing attack that Army could not check and gave the midshipmen a two-touchdown margin once more. From that time on, Sadecky's Bandits barred the gates, but Army's Go-Go team could add but three more points before the final gun sounded. Navy had made it four straight, and the cadets poured out of the stadium with their heads still up, and their shoulders thrown back, but their pride somewhat bent.

"We'll get 'em next year," Lew Sistak shouted, above the racket made by the exit of a hundred thousand spectators.

There were tears of frustration in his dark eyes. "We'll have Lee and Schaye again next year. They're losing their whole first-string backfield, and four standout linemen."

A plebe yelled, "I'm from Brooklyn! I'm used to waiting until next year."

Ron was thinking mostly of the long-distance call he would put through to Grantwood when he got to the Bellevue-Stratford. Army had lost a football game again, and so cadets were really not supermen after all. Maybe they served rarer steaks to the men of Crabtown.

It was getting well on toward five-thirty before he heard his mother's voice. "Everybody's just fine, Ron. Yes, we saw part of the game, and we're sorry Army had to lose. It was silly, I know, but we tried to pick you out of all those cadets when they marched in. Those close-ups on TV surely didn't give me the impression that any of the cadets are mistreated. Oh, Sally is thrilled with your letters. . . . Dad? He's the same as usual. I'll put him on."

"Hello there, son. How goes it?"

"It isn't a piece of cake, believe me," Ron said. "Not as easy as I had it at home. I've drawn a lot of demerits because of the way I was allowed to get away with murder as a kid."

"Look, *I* did some time in the service, son. You can't always get away with passing the buck. You had a knack of——"

"Time's running out, Dad. Put Mother back on."

He listened to the motherly advice as old as the hills. Take care of himself, and remember that he was susceptible to chest colds. "Sure, Mom," he ribbed, "the red flag flies when it's time to put on the red flannels, and there's one sure thing—they can't catch me in the draft."

Along with Lew and Leo, he toured the crowded downtown area of the city and admittedly basked in the admiring glances of the civilians, particularly those of the younger and gentler sex. They managed to get some theater tickets, made available to the visiting cadets and midshipmen far in advance, and saw the road show of a popular Broadway musical. It was nearly midnight when they returned to their hotel room. Lew Sistak heaved a deep sigh as he peeled off. "Now I know how Cinderella felt. It has been a *ball*. If only the ball had bounced the right way for us this afternoon!"

"The Navy guys we met," Leo said, "didn't rub it in at all. They were real nice guys."

"Why do you suppose they are where they are?" Lew queried.

"Yeah," Ron said after a yawn, then let his thoughts drift ahead. Most of the big Rabble would leave the training table, at least for a while, and changes of personnel at each table in the mess hall would be made. The changes were a matter of policy at the academy every few weeks, to establish closer personal contacts in the corps and to lessen the possibilities of personal conflicts that are apt to arise wherever men are thrown together. Where would they sit Second Classman Jason Lee? Far, far away, Ron hoped and prayed.

"That touchdown we should have had," Lew said. "A man in the hotel lobby said the replay camera showed that Donnmyer's feet *were* in bounds when he caught that pass in the third quarter. It could have made things different."

"We haven't any B-aches," Leo Ralston replied. "The referee, when we were moving that time, missed a clipping call. I saw Trowbridge cut down that Navy blocker from behind. Everything evens up, as a rule. The only mistake Army made was not having Ballinger kidnaped two days before the game. He's a junior Y. A. Tittle."

It was a gloomy Sabbath back on the banks of the Hudson. Even the long-eared equine mascots, the poop had it, hardly sniffed at their oats and hay, and before the lights went out, that night, rumors that Sadecky had had it at West Point were already stirring. In their Sunday stints, the football experts inferred that Orv Richler would have done much better if he had been allowed to be his own man. At West Point, however, you obeyed orders, first, last, and always.

Lew Sistak snorted with disgust when he read one of the stories. "Hogwash! Those jugheads are down the tubes. They're from hunger."

Ron was not so sure. In fact, he was not quite sure of anything since that phone call home.

CHAPTER EIGHT

Turkey day came and as swiftly passed by, and soon the first real snow of the year blanketed the reservation, and the plebes began calling off the days to the Christmas holidays. Their longing for family firesides was tempered by the realization that they would "own" the academy during the days the upperclassmen were on leave. Brightly wrapped packages began to arrive at the barracks, their contents naturally restricted to things to chew on or articles necessary to maintain the spit and polish image of the cadets. Ron opened a package from Sally Bradley and laid bare an initialed gold tie clasp he could not hope to use for at least eight years.

"You hang on to it," Leo said. "The way they're emptying Fort Knox, you could make a profit some day."

Lew Sistak untangled a fruit cake from its wrappings and hefted it in his hands. "As heavy as a Tac officer's heart," he said, and brought it close to his nose. "Wow! It is also loaded—and not with lemonade! Good old Aunt Sophie. The barracks police are going to have a ball."

"She should have hidden a saw in it," Ron said.

"Escape from here? You kidding, Ron? I never had it so good." Lew wiped a grin from his face and studied his roommate for a moment. "You're still homesick!" He swung his eyes toward Leo, and the plebe shook his head.

"I learned to stand on my own feet a long time ago, Lew. At sixteen my mother told me I was to take over as the man of the house. I did the marketing, and I made my own bed, and while my mother was working I cooked my own meals."

Ron laughed out of one corner of his mouth. "So you were never homesick, either one of you. Just sick of home." He put his head down. "I didn't mean that. You're a couple of lucky stiffs."

"I think I know what you mean," Lew said, "but are you putting all the blame where it maybe doesn't belong, Ron?"

"I should study myself in the mirror?"

Sistak shook his head. "Wouldn't do you any good. You wouldn't see what the Tac officers most likely have seen already. They'll let you know, soon enough."

"Let's forget the riddles," Leo said. "God rest ye merry, gentlemen, let nothing you dismay—let's all keep our spirits up, until Foundation Day!"

The ice broke and melted into laughter.

The nerve-wracking and solemn occasion took place a few days after the three upper classes returned from Christmas leave. From the poop deck of the mess hall, the adjutant of the corps, in an appropriately funereal voice, called off the names of all cadets who had been "found"—those who had failed to make the required 2.0 passing mark in recitation and those who had flunked the semiannual examination after two tries.

Not even the semblance of a smile was visible in the sea of cadet faces. This was heartbreak, frustration, and a terrible blow to pride. Ron had played football with and against seven of the unfortunates, and as the names were called they hit him as hard as a physical blow. One thing he was at last sure of after "Battalions rise!" and that was that he no longer wanted "out" of West Point—at least, not at the request of the Superintendent. There was a great difference between getting fired and resigning.

Looking up from his studying later, Sistak said, "Did you know there was a yearling in that bunch with an average of better than two point five? Deficiency in conduct. Lack of aptitude for the Army. He belongs in Princeton or Harvard."

"You don't have to remind me," Ron said stiffly. "I'll watch my step."

"Man, you're really a sensitive type! Every time I throw a shoe, you try it on to see if it fits."

Ron let the matter drop and gave his attention to the last issue of *The Pointer*. The "Barrow-graph" said that Army was still stinging over the defeat by Navy on the gridiron but was getting a measure of revenge in the lesser sports. Army's big five had beaten the Crabtown cagers, 92 to 71, only a few days ago, and West Point's wrestlers had dumped the Middies. The one increasing purpose, however, as far as the corps was concerned, was to stop Navy's winning streak at Philadelphia come another November.

"Sadecky's material for next fall, as it stands for the moment," the cadet scribe wrote, "seems far superior to Eddleston's at Annapolis. Whit Blum proved he was heir apparent to Richler's quarterback spot during the last three games of last year, and in the backfield Sadecky will have a hard-running back who has come into his own, Jason Lee. Brick-horn, a fine blocking back, and Mr. Outside, Joe Scott, still have another year to settle accounts with Navy. Only four of the Bandits' first string will graduate in June. Three of last fall's plebe team have a chance to make the big Rabble, Frank Troy told your correspondent the other day. Army's skaters ran over Massachusetts for the second time, peppering their goalie with a 11-to-2 win.

"Down at Annapolis next autumn, the cry will be 'Make It Five!' and here at the Point it will be 'Four and *No More!*' The intramural basketball league is red hot as usual, and company teams are as bent on winning as the Army big five and want that honored championship designation on the intramural plaque in the gymnasium. . . ."

"You know something?" Lew said. "I won't be much over twenty-six when I'm through with the Army. That is, if I want to be. How old was Y. A. Tittle and that Bednarik when they quit pro football?"

Cadet Ralston glanced toward Ron and shook his head. "And we thought he was dedicated to the military, the big faker. If an autopsy was performed on him, you'd find lacings in his heart. If you ever make the Bandits, I'll push a peanut across Central Area with my nose."

"I'm holding you to that. And with that nose, Leo, you won't have too difficult a time."

After taps, Ron lay awake for over an hour, plagued by feelings of misgiving. He wondered why. His marks were holding steady, and he could think of no reason why his name would be on the delinquency reports the Tac officers were making ready. . . . Less than twenty-four hours later he had the answer. The personnel at the tables in the mess hall had been shuffled, and he found himself sitting at a table across from Second Classman Jason Lee. The big meat pie had hardly been placed on the table when the fullback said, his eyes fixed sternly on Ron, "Company C lost a basketball game to Company G yesterday, Mister. We're not happy about it. Cheer us up, Mister. And tuck that chin in where it belongs! You're taking up too much of your chair, Mister!"

Ron had to think fast. "Sir, there was a sheepherder in Wyoming who couldn't find any shepherds, so he went to Spain and hired three Basques. He brought them to the States and took them to a big New York hotel. While he was registering they started having a ball in the revolving doors, and they finally spun themselves out in the street and were run over by a truck. Sir, the moral is—don't ever put all your Basques in one exit."

Small smiles of appreciation flitted across the faces of the upperclassmen. A plebe sitting at the table commandant's right hand nearly turned blue, fighting to control his appreciation of the contribution, and Cadet Lee quickly snapped, "Turn gray, Mister! We're not partial to Navy blue."

By the time the big dish of Jello capped with whipped cream was served, Ron had fought back the almost uncontrollable urge to feed the upperclassman personally, to let him wear his dessert instead of eating it. Why had the cadet always seemed to have chosen him as a pet target? Some day he would meet the man far beyond the limits of the reservation. Then—Pow!

That afternoon between classes he read another letter from Sally Bradley, and it gave his morale anything but a lift. The girl wrote that she heard from Eddie Lowden often and that he was doing fine at Penn State. Hadn't he always?

Most of what she had written he absorbed abstractedly, and he quickly reached for his pen. The answer to the letter consumed half of his study period. He had never been able to compete with Eddie, and even wearing the uniform of a West Point cadet he did not believe his chances were any better, even if a doting mother thought otherwise. Maybe he would see her when he went home next June.

Leaving his last class that afternoon, he regretted having mailed the letter but could not give himself a clear reason why, and passing Jason Lee and another upperclassman on the stairway in the barracks he wondered why he felt another foot shorter. Maybe he should tell his mother when he wrote home again what that cadet officer had said about trying to make something in four years that should have been in production eighteen years before. "Would you believe it?" he'd write, "I really believe they classify me as one of their problem children here at the academy. An overgrown Army brat."

"I find the uniform hasn't changed you a bit," Sally wrote him a week later. "With you it has always had to be clear sailing all the way, or you wouldn't play. I thought my letters would help you over the rough spots, but I see I have wasted my time. Your mother never had anything to do with my writing you in the first place, and get it out of your head that she spoiled you. You did the complete job on yourself. I wish you luck, for you're going to need it."

"Am I wrong in guessing that's a 'Dear John' letter?" Lew asked. "I think I read the signs."

Ron nodded, managed a grin. "It's just as well, Lew. One woman is enough right now in my life."

"You got a real bad break in life, didn't you? But I just can't bleed for you. The break was you were not born an orphan, Ron. Just what kind of a crutch are you leaning on? You'd better throw it away pretty soon, or you'll always be a cripple above the ears."

"Go back to the books. You need 'em," Ron fired back.

The days that followed were like all days in a plebe's life. The days rolled into weeks and resolved into months, and by the time Recognition Day arrived, Ron's urge for retaliation overwhelmed him. Only a few days ago he had completed a punishment tour in the Central Area, and it had stuck in his mind that Jason Lee could well have been responsible for it. Well, on a certain fine day in June the tables would be turned. On Recognition Day the plebes preside as first classmen at the tables in the mess hall, and real first classmen traditionally cater to their wishes and serve the food. Amiably they take what they have dished out to the plebes for the past eleven months, while the officer on the poop deck sees only what he wants to see.

Cadet Sid Burnett, the "table commandant," put Jason Lee in charge of the "cow," the milk pitcher. "What is a cow, Mister?" he asked a cadet, in a voice that was meant to be stern.

"Sir," the upperclassman replied, "she walks, she talks, she's full of chalk; the lacteal fluid extracted from the female of the bovine species is highly prolific to the nth degree."

"Thanks, Mister. You may sit at ease while you have dessert."

Ron, a few seconds later, began his revenge on Jason Lee. "I see no wrinkles in that chin, Mister! Throw your shoulders back and bring your gut in! You're using all of your chair, Mister Dumbguard. It is not a camp stool. The edge of your chair, Mister. No, that's not enough—come on, on the skin edge. That's b——"

There was a crash as the chair and Jason Lee suddenly parted company. An outbreak of laughter in the immediate area was short-lived when the second classman got slowly to his feet and gave evidence that he was in some pain. A cadet slid his chair back under him. Jason Lee, little globules of sweat forming around his mouth, picked up Ron with his eyes. "You have been trained well for the Beast Detail, Mister!" He squirmed in his chair. "Whew, that floor came up hard!"

Ron felt the critical pressure of many pairs of eyes. They were telling him that he had shown spite and had not entered into the true spirit of the occasion and, worse, that he had risked damage to one of the academy's most valuable football assets. "Sir," he leveled at Lee, "I'm sorry."

"Table Commandant" Burnett said, "I wish to apologize for all us slaves so graciously released from bondage."

A first classman wearing a battalion commander's stripes said to no one in particular, "There have been men who graduated from West Point still plebes under their skins. The purpose of the discipline here never quite registered inside their heads."

Ron's ears burned. He wished the chair under him would collapse, along with the floor.

For the rest of the day the grapevine buzzed. The poop had it that Jason Lee had been checked up at the cadet hospital, but no serious injury had been apparent.

"Man," Lew said to Ron, "you would have had to resign if there had been! Either that or go through the next three years below the status of the Superintendent's dog. Boy, it felt wonderful at my table, the way the upperclassmen showed their true feelings. Bygones *were* bygones."

"So I goofed," Ron admitted. "Let's drop it right there."

"Imagine, thirty days' leave! Then *we yearlings* give a

hearty welcome to the new bunch of plebes. Then Camp Buckner and football practice." Cadet Sistak fell on his bed and kicked up his heels.

Ron caught himself about to tell Lew he had not exactly bought any more of the Military Academy, that he would have to think it over carefully during the next thirty days. He was certain he could not place better than twenty-four hundredth if they ran a personality contest at the academy. The clapboard house back in Grantwood was more than a home to go to at the moment; it was a sanctuary.

He caught himself about to strike a brace when three upperclassmen entered the room, one of them Cadet Captain Yale Gambrun, the big gun of last year's Army team. Gambrun congratulated Ron, then quickly turned toward Lew. "You looked good in spring practice, Sistak, and you've got an even chance to make the big Rabble. Coach Troy is high on you, and Ray Sadecky seldom if ever questions his judgment. I wish I had another year here. I never was on a team that beat Navy."

When the cadets left, Lew Sistak's eyes were as bright as a polished "fried egg," the headpiece on a shako. "That's the kind of guy he is, Ron! He takes the time to make the rounds congratulating the likes of us."

"You, not *us*," Ron corrected. "Just a future football hero." He crossed the room and stared out into the semi-darkness. "I don't see any instructors on the way here to pay me a visit, despite my two point six average. The big A on a sweater means Army football, *not* academics."

"Yale Gambrun's A means both, don't you forget that, Ron. He topped you in tougher subjects in the classrooms with a two point seven and a little better, so stow that away in your stubborn head. When it comes to putting out with the muscle instead of brains, you want it without trying too

92

hard, on a silver platter. I watched you playing football. When you got hit you were satisfied to stay hit. There's an old saying, 'Let George do it,' but when he does, the buck-passers dislike him and envy his ability."

"That sermon, Lew, was almost as good as the one by the chaplain last Sunday."

Lew grinned and threw up his hands. "O.K., my friend, you stick to your religion and I'll hang on to mine." He turned a little solemn. "You and me and Leo got along pretty good this past year, but one thing bothered me: I was afraid we would get to look alike. Next year who will we have to get used to?"

"I'll cross that bridge if I come to it," Ron said.

"Be sure it's one built by the Army engineers," Lew replied.

CHAPTER NINE

The little part of the world that was Grantwood, Pennsylvania, looked almost strange to the cadet when he got off the bus in front of Hall's Drugstore, as if he had only passed through it at one time. It should have seemed smaller on his return, he thought, but it seemed larger. Aware of the attention he drew, he walked two blocks to Burritt's Hardware Store and found it busier than he ever remembered it to be. His father, that easy-going man, seemed to be waiting on three customers all at once, and he was talking and laughing. Ten minutes later his father was driving him home.

"So it was that rough, was it?" Harvey Burritt asked his son. "Well, whatever they do to a kid there, I'm for it one hundred per cent. You're an inch taller, and you've put on weight you really needed."

After Ron had been at home two hours, he wondered at the reaction to his tales of near mental torture at West

Point. His parents listened and studied him closely, but without any outward signs of compassion. Then his father interrupted him. "They say that once you have hurdled the first year, the rest can be taken in stride."

"I doubt very much if I want any more," Ron said flatly. "I've just about decided to resign."

"So you're quitting again," his mother said, and quietly shook her head.

"What do you mean—again?" the cadet asked, his temper heating. "You pushed me into something I wasn't ready for! You——"

"Couldn't they teach you manners at West Point either?" his father wanted to know. "Ron, what have you been making up inside your head while you've been feeling sorry for yourself? You never finished anything you ever started if it looked too tough."

He sat there, altogether bewildered, as his father erased the image he had made for himself, to suit only himself, during the last eleven months. It had been the competition, not the coach, that had scared him off the high school team. The opposition got a lot of shots at a man carrying the ball. When he'd had chores to do, like mowing the lawn or shoveling snow, he'd managed to get a pain somewhere. Once beaten he refused to try again. They had about given up on him when the miracle came to pass, the appointment to West Point as an alternate. Thank heavens he had never let the textbooks lick him, and that outwardly his character could not be questioned.

"Ron," his mother said, offering him a comforting smile, "Dad is right. You took advantage of us, knowing we would never lay a hand on you. The more we tried to talk to you, the less you would listen, and we finally threw up our hands. The complaining letters you wrote had us terribly worried, but the fact that you stuck it out during the difficult first year is proof that you can do anything you want to if you try hard enough. Truthfully, I see a great change in you, even if you don't see or feel it yourself."

Ron, staring at the floor, felt like somebody coming out of a trance. He knew now why he had felt a little scared getting off the bus. He had come back to where the real truth was. He lifted his eyes to meet those of his parents. "That roommate I had at the academy—I mentioned him in my letters—Lew Sistak. He was a lot smarter than I thought."

"You're going to Rotary with me tomorrow, son," Harvey Burritt said, and leaned forward and laid a hand on Ron's shoulder. "I'm going to be mighty proud to show you off!"

The thirty days passed only too swiftly. Soon Ron found himself at Camp Buckner, the summer camp ten miles from West Point, renewing old ties with Lew Sistak, Wahoo Mc-Grath, Leo Ralston, and many other new yearlings. He found himself part of the Beast Detail, assigned to taking the rough civilian edges off the new class of plebes, and, recognizing certain weaknesses in many of them that he had had a year ago himself, he felt no compunction about putting on the pressure.

"I wondered how I'd feel with the shoe on the other foot," Lew said after mess one day. "If I'd feel sorry for the plebes. I don't, not a bit."

The new yearlings had their own cross to bear. Under the hot August sun they were put through a punishing course in tactical training by officers of the regular Army and a group of first classmen. The course embraced periods of instruction in the combat branches of Artillery, Infantry,

Armor, Engineers, Signal, and combat support branches of Transportation and Quartermaster. In between times, however, there was time for swimming in Lake Popolopen, and drags were allowed to grace picnics of a Sunday. On Saturday night there were hops at Doris Barth Hall. Sports of all kinds were a must.

The second year at the Military Academy, Ron thought, was not going to be too hard to take, until one late afternoon coming off the field after booting a soccer ball around he heard his name called in a voice that rang of first-class authority. He swung his glance toward three husky sun-tanned cadets clad only in shorts and basketball shoes. Their eyes, probing him, were not friendly and reminded him of so many delinquency reports. He walked over to the trio. "You called me?" he asked, then recognized one of them, Joe Scott, Army halfback.

"We thought you'd might like to know," Cadet Scott said. "I got a letter from Jason Lee yesterday, Burritt. From West Germany, where he's been attached to an armored division. He's having trouble with his back, and he's afraid he's going to be slowed up a little this fall if it doesn't leave him. Looks like that last Recognition Day was one that cost Army plenty. When Sadecky hears about it, and the rest of the corps, you're not going to be the most popular cadet at the academy."

"It was an accident, you know that," Ron replied, a sinking feeling in his stomach. "Something could have happened to him over there—how do we know?"

Scott shook his head. "Ever since you caused him to hit the floor that day, Burritt, he's had trouble. Do us a favor and volunteer for Sadecky's B squad!"

"I might do that, Mister Scott!" Ron shot back, then

abruptly gave the first classman his back and walked away.

"Maybe they'll give you the Navy Cross!" one of the cadets shouted after him.

That night, on duty in the guard tent, he dismally contemplated the chicken that had come home to roost, the stiff price it seemed he would have to pay for one brief moment of satisfaction in the mess hall last June. In a week's time the football summer camp would open, and candidates for the big Rabble would report to Ray Sadecky and his staff. Without a fullback of the caliber of the departed Yale Gambrun, Army's chances of beating half of the teams on the fall schedule, to say nothing of turning the tables on Navy, would be slim indeed. He felt right now as if the Bat Board had the right to shoot him at sunrise.

The following afternoon at the Lake, washing off the sweat and strain of field maneuvers, he gave Wahoo, Lew, and Willie Drumm the poop according to First Classman Joe Scott.

"That's a wicked spot to put anybody on," Lew commiserated. "After all, you didn't *pull* his chair out from under him. And who knows but what he hurt himself over in Germany? Boy, if he's that bad, Army will have a rough time of it. In spring practice, the offensive backfield behind Lee and Scott looked pretty thin. The yearlings that came out looked as green as grass. And you know Chuck Frohmeyer never got by Foundation Day last January."

"It all could be grossly exaggerated," Wahoo observed, as the four cadets made their way toward the area occupied by Company C. On a wide field off to the right, a bunch of cadets were playing soccer, and the ball came sailing toward the road. Ron put on a burst of speed, caught it on the bounce, and boomed it back in bounds. Lew and the others froze in their tracks. "And with sneakers on?" Wahoo gasped. A jeep came up and the colonel ordered his cadet driver to stop. "What is your name, Mister?" he asked Ron.

"Burritt, Sir. Third classman."

"You really put your toe into that ball, Burritt. Sadecky loves kickers." He grinned, then ordered his driver to move on.

"Hiding your light under a bushel, huh?" Sistak said.

"Maybe soccer's the game I'm fitted for, Lew."

"Could be. It needs a hard head." He appraised his fellow cadet out of the corner of his eye as they approached First Battalion headquarters. "You've grown an inch since I first met you, and I'll bet you're a few pounds heavier. Why not give it another try at the football camp?"

"Look, Lew, I wouldn't have a ghost of a chance for the big Rabble."

"That's plebe talk, wouldn't you say, Wahoo?" Sistak said. "Who said you *could* make the corps team? But Sadecky has to have football players to help develop the ones who can."

Ron felt a small shudder run through him. "You mean the B squad? The Band-Aids? Lew, I'll volunteer for any jungle war that's going on, but—well, I'll think about it."

He did no more than that during the last week in August, despite Lew's prodding. The night before the cadets were to break summer camp and move back to West Point, Sistak, already bearing slight scars of contact, put a bee in his ear. "Jim Buschere took me aside today. He's the offensive backfield coach. 'This cadet Burritt,' he said. 'Colonel Crowe told me something about him kicking a soccer ball a country mile. Why isn't he here? He played intramural last year.' "

"Things get around, don't they, Lew? Like Jason Lee's poor aching back. A good many of the cadets here are avoiding me as if I had leprosy."

"You still can make it, Ron. There's almost three weeks to the opener with Boston College." Sistak settled down on his cot and bit some loose skin off a knuckle. "We had it all the way today. Stance and shoulder blocking, defensive charge, blocking and tackling, team organization, and play development. Sadecky got more bad news today. Mitch Ohl, the guy who was expected to play behind Joe Scott, broke a leg in a jeep accident in Belgium."

"The head coaches always make things sound worse than they really are," Ron argued. "It's a kind of alibi in advance, not that I blame them. Winning is their bread and butter."

"All right," Lew said, under his breath, "I wish you luck playing volleyball and ping-pong."

The entire corps, including upperclassmen who had served overseas during the summer, began another year at West Point in September. Ron drew Willie Drumm and a yearling named Jud Pittman for roommates. At the cadet store, the day after the new plebes had been duly presented to the corps, Ron got the poop on Jason Lee. The fullback was at the cadet hospital getting a thorough checkup while Ray Sadecky paced the floor of his office in the gymnasium, drinking black coffee by the quart.

It felt good to be a third classman. No more marching to classes, no square corners, a few more minutes of sleep in the morning, and complete ease at the mess tables. Ron's touch of euphoria, however, was of short duration. The information from the hospital was that Sadecky's star fullback had some sort of displacement in the lumbar region, and his durability through the tough Army football schedule was a question mark. He was quoted as saying he would give it a try all the way.

Wherever Ron went the first three days after leaving summer camp, he read his questionable status in the eyes of scores of cadets. They seemed to tell him he was still a plebe in a yearling's uniform, a deserter to the Navy. They inferred that he had incurred a debt he was going to have to pay one way or another. Things began to look as dismal as they had a year ago, until one night he received a visitor.

He was scanning the pages of a calculus book when Cadet Captain Jason Lee entered the room. Involuntarily he got to his feet and threw his shoulders back.

"At ease, Burritt," Lee said, and sat down in Willie Drumm's chair. "I understand you're getting treated to a kind of Coventry."

"Something like that," Ron said. "I'll never get over being sorry for what happened last——"

"It really wasn't your fault," Lee said. "Just an unfortunate accident. I believe I'll do all right in spite of it. And I am going to do my best to get you off a hook you don't deserve to be on."

"I wouldn't belong here, Jase," Ron said, "if I denied I didn't put some of my spleen behind the going over I gave you last June."

"Don't give that to *The Pointer,* Burritt," the cadet captain said, smiling. "Confession, though, is good for the soul. There's one thing you *can* do to ease your mind, and that is to come out to Daly Field tomorrow afternoon and help the big Rabble get ready. It'll be tough, but I don't know of a better penance for a guy in your situation. Of course, I can't order you to play football, Burritt. That's entirely up to you. But I don't know of any other sport, offhand, that tests a man's character so well and sifts out the defects."

Ron stared at the wall for a long time after the first

classman had left the room. He knew he had been pleasantly reminded of his duty and shown the best way he could live with himself during the months ahead. Jason Lee, without a doubt, was the whole man they strove to perfect at West Point, one, he was sure, who would wear the five-pointed star of the distinguished cadet before a new year came around.

He knew what he had to do. No weaseling out now. He could smell the medication, the oil of wintergreen, and the rubbing alcohol in the trainer's room. The whirlpool baths were spinning in front of his eyes, he felt the tape tighten at his knees and ankles, and there was a taste of salt in his mouth. He'd let the big Army team run over him day by day and try to have enough left to play with Company C in the intramurals on Fridays.

That night he went over to the Second and Third Class Club in Mahan Hall with Willie Drumm and half a dozen other cadets to get the first taste of how the other half relaxed at the academy. There were billiard tables, and a hi-fi, and deep lounge chairs. He met Lew and Wahoo there and told them that he had put himself up as a martyr to the cause— on one condition. "If I make the supreme sacrifice, you write the sad letter home."

Lew held out his hand. "I knew you wouldn't chicken out on me. And bear in mind that the mortality rate among the little Rabble comes to nothing but a few broken ribs, some missing teeth, and slight concussions of the brain."

"How can I thank you for such reassurance, Lew?" Ron said, forcing a grin. "I wish you the same luck."

"He didn't tell you," Wahoo cut in, "that he has a good chance of playing with the big boys. When he blocks and tackles he hasn't a friend in the world. So say good-by to him until Thanksgiving Day." He selected a cue from the rack and asked for suckers to please volunteer. "You tell Ron, Lew?"

"Brickhorn is the only guy who can boot the ball to suit Sadecky this year," Sistak said. "Just after the first workout here, Sadecky wanted to know about a yearling by the name of 'Bertitz' or 'Bowitt' or some such name. Colonel Crowe had mentioned that the cadet could possibly be a sleeper."

"The brass doesn't miss a thing, does it?" Ron muttered under his breath.

"You surprised me, too," Lew told him. "Not only the distance you kicked that big melon, but the speed you made cutting it off. Well, *we* can use you, when we work on rushing the kicker. You'll find the turf out there pretty soft yet, so there's no sweat."

"You forget, Lew. I'm a tackle."

"Last year you were a plebe, too."

Ron made an attempt to play some pool but he soon gave up. There was too much nervous moisture in the palms of his hands, and the ivory balls assumed the faces of giant Black Knights with gleaming eyes loaded with mayhem. He would talk it over with himself again after taps and see if he could think up a good reason to change his mind. Leaving Mahan Hall with Wahoo and Willie, he knew he had completely run out of excuses during his little over nineteen years. "Wahoo," he said, in a voice that hardly sounded like his own, "we'll see how hard they fall tomorrow."

"I saw—last spring, during twenty workouts," Cadet McGrath said. "Brother, they *hit!* Sadecky picked his thirty-three starters, and out of them he has only fourteen lettermen. I think I've got an outside chance of staying with the A squad, but I'm battling a first classman for that end spot.

The coach is worried over his favorite offensive weapon, the toe. He's looking for a punter and a placement kicker. Well, we'll have a pretty good line again, especially at the tackles. Whit Blum and Harry Dreyer, the quarterbacks. Steve Borek hurt his knee last spring and—"

Ron barely heard Wahoo's analysis of Army's material. He was not just an ordinary bright-eyed and bushy-tailed cadet offering Sadecky his services. He was *that* cadet named Burritt, and he had but one comforting thought: the head coach had not graduated from West Point. Willie Drumm exploded that thought. "Jim Buschere and Nick Aronian know their business all right. They're both West Point graduates."

Cadet Ronald Burritt reached for a line in the Cadet Prayer to sustain him. *Make us choose the harder right instead of the easier wrong, and never to be content with a half truth when the whole can be won.*

At breakfast the next morning, he caught himself feeling sorry for the two plebes at his table who were getting the full treatment from Joe Scott and a second classman, and then he realized what it could cost him for having been sorry for himself, and he got into the needling ritual on his own.

"Do you like it here, Mister?" he asked.

"Yes, Sir!"

Ron groaned inwardly. That wrong answer meant more disciplinary pressure, for no plebe could be considered truthful—or even human—who admitted to liking his first year at the Military Academy.

Out of the collar of his gray uniform, the neophyte asked permission to speak. The request granted, he said in a voice badly in need of lubrication, "Sir, I wish to correct that statement. I hate it here."

"That's much better, Mister."

Leaving the mess hall, Ron felt a fluttering sensation in his stomach. The shrill sound of a whistle muffled the sound of hundreds of moving feet. Classes would not start until Monday. It promised to be a long and rugged afternoon at Daly Field.

CHAPTER TEN

At three o'clock that afternoon, on Daly Field, screened from the outside world, Army Head Coach Ray Sadecky, flanked by two of his staff, took his first look at the sacrificial lambs, the Green Hornets and the Band-Aids that made up the B squad. Ron, wearing a pot-luck uniform, felt more scared than he had the day he'd braced in front of a first classman for the first time. Sadecky always had a comforting word for these invaluable players. They were essential to his success at West Point.

"Like a lot of roses," he began his welcoming remarks, "you men are born to blush unseen. You get no headlines, and you get no outward credit when the big Rabble wins. But always bear in mind that you'll be an essential part of every Army victory. It's going to be a lot of sweat and take up much of your time here at the academy. We will dress you up as the enemy almost every afternoon from now until the season's over. You'll run Boston College's offense against us until the opening game, and you'll put up their defense against the big Rabble's attack, the Go-Go team. You will go at full speed and charge hard on the defense, avoiding, of course, any unnecessary roughness."

He paused and ran his eyes over the human guinea pigs.

"We're going to dispense with a lot of useless preliminaries and start out *playing* football. All of you have played intramural ball, and it goes without saying that West Point cadets are always in condition. One more thing. You can never tell where a blister will rise. How do we know there isn't a sleeper or two among you who could make the A squad? Haven't there been occasions here at the Point when a plebe has been recognized long before Recognition Day?"

Assistant Coach Buschere buzzed Sadecky's ear, and the coach nodded.

"I won't under any circumstances allow any personal vendettas to be settled on this field, and I'm telling every man here to completely ignore certain poop that's been going around."

Ron stared straight ahead, feeling as conspicuous as a spotted white dog on a fiery red wagon, but inwardly he thanked Sadecky. The other coaches arrived with the Army trainer, Bert Gorman, and Sadecky gave instructions to Buschere and Aronian to sift out the best in the B squad as fast as possible.

It was part of a coach's job to keep a book on football talent at the academy, even among the players involved in the intramural league. Ron's name was not mentioned when the tackles were singled out. When Nick Aronian lined his men up for stance correction, Buschere came over and called him out of the player pool. "Burritt, you played company football as a tackle. You weren't one of the best."

"Coach, I admit it."

"I've heard you are fast on your feet and can kick. We need a wingback on the Green Hornets, the offensive B squad. Let me see your hands."

Ron held them out.

"You'll do," Buschere said. "You'll be the backfield, along with Sid Burnett, Russ Kirsch, and Jud Pittman. You know those cadets?"

"All but Kirsch," Ron said.

The big Rabble worked on play development that hot afternoon, the maroon-jerseyed Band-Aids getting their baptism. The Green Hornets were ridden hard as they tried to polish up an offense against a ragtag line of intramuralists so as to insure the big Army team's defense against reasonable opposition when deadly serious work began. Ron discovered that a convert from tackle to wingback was no small piece of cake. Why hadn't he let the soccer ball alone that day? But the feel of the football in his hands gave him an incentive he'd never had before. You knew you had to carry it somewhere. You had the feeling that part of the game was in your hands.

Buschere's tongue had an appropriate sting as he drove his Hornets. He concentrated mostly on building up a green halfback, just enough, he told Ron during a breather, to let him stay alive. "The fact you can run might be your life insurance, Burritt."

After an hour and a half, he seemed to float in his sweat. The coach's voice crisscrossed through his brain.

"Make use of your fakes, feints, and false starts! Make use of your interference, Burritt! Never change your position for starting. The pivot step is slow time, the cross-over just the opposite! Burritt, you knucklehead!"

Buschere finally called a halt and singled out Ron and Sid Burnett.

"Let's see if you *can* boot the ball, Burritt."

Ron was both dog-tired and nervous. His first kick carried a little over thirty-five yards. Burnett booted one for forty. Buschere picked up another ball and held it up in front of Ron's nose. "Keep your eye on the ball until you kick it, and extend the toe and snap your leg. Hit the ball with the outside instep. Always follow through with left arm extended. Try it again."

The cadet breathed in deep and took a look around to steady himself down. Not fifty feet away, Ray Sadecky, his hands on his hips, was watching. Ron put his foot into the ball, with everything he had left in his weary frame, and boomed it for a good fifty yards. Sadecky came over and studied Ron for a moment. "Maybe the colonel was right," he said, addressing Buschere. Giving the B-squad player his attention again, he seemed less impressed. "Burritt, it can be a lot different under pressure, when half a dozen big linemen are trying to get at you."

"I imagine so," Ron said, his throat dry.

"Keep working on him, Jim," Sadecky said and walked back to give the lash to the big Rabble.

Ron swore he would not need any whip. It was known by all sports authorities that Ray Sadecky set tremendous store by the kicking game, that there had to be a good reason for the "foot" in football. The opening kickoff had been the difference in a score many times, and he considered the punt one of the finest offensive weapons in the game.

Buschere grinned and slapped Ron on the shoulder. "O.K., let's stop dreaming, Cinderella. Let's see you do better by about five yards. With the pressure on." He threw up a line and ordered the "defense" to get in on the kicker. Ron stepped back ten yards, took a high pass from his center, and had to kick in a hurry. The punt was almost blocked and traveled only about twenty yards. "You'll be gun-shy for a while," the coach said. "The A squad will cure you of it or kill you."

In the gym, cleaned of his sweat and getting into his uniform, Ron shed himself of illusions. It was one thing for Jason Lee to forgive and forget, but the mass thinking of the corps was something else again. It was possible for a cadet to graduate from West Point with the doubtful distinction of having caused Navy to defeat Army for five straight years. Despite Sadecky's subtle reference to reprisals, he felt certain many of the Army regulars knew how to hit a man full blast without seeming to do so. The old temptation to quit was strong inside him when his roommate, Jud Pittman, shouted above the racket in the locker room, "You know, we were pretty good out there today. I wonder how it will feel to dump one of the big team?"

Ron gave the Green Hornet fullback a wry look. "You came to the right place to ask. I can tell you it doesn't feel good. In my case it could get a lot worse."

"I think you're taking that too seriously," Pittman said. "Lee didn't look much like a cripple to me today."

"He hasn't had to go all out yet, Jud."

Outside the gym, he found Lew Sistak and Wahoo waiting. Lew, when they were well on the way to the barracks, gave out some information that bid fair to spoil his supper. "Lee's wearing a kind of corset. I don't have to tell you this is top secret. If the Eagles from Boston find that out they'll surely dig their claws into him." He nudged his old roommate in the ribs. "I heard you buzzed pretty good out there."

Ron shrugged. "One swallow doesn't make a man a candidate for Alcoholics Anonymous."

Three days later the wraps were off, and Sadecky had B squad's Hornets banging away inside and outside the tackle spots, with Ron and Sid Burnett doing most of the carrying and getting lessons in defensive line play from the rugged Bandits. Working from an analysis of the films of last year's game against Boston College, Sadecky's orders for the Hornets were to employ the Eagle shifts and put a man in motion. He had the "enemy" defensive ends split wide from the tackles into better pass-catching locations. He had the guards shifting laterally along with the tackles, varying the gap between their positions, the better to set up better blocking angles.

Russ Kirsch, quarterbacking for the little Rabble, sent Ron on an attempted sweep of the Bandits' left end, and he wondered where his blockers were just before he was clobbered by the whole left side of the big defensive line. His breath gushed out when he hit the ground, and he was certain a big hand came down on his helmet and pushed his face into the turf for good measure. Two big Bandits helped him to his feet. "You outran your blockers, Burritt," one of them said. "That could be unhealthy."

Buschere echoed the Bandits' criticism before calling another play. Ron, as Kirsch called the signals, ran laterally toward the side line, the man in motion. From his flanker position he faked moving downfield, then cut back in to block the Bandits' defensive end, a two-hundred-and-ten-pound cadet, Benny Haag. Something like a tank must have hit him, he thought. While they hauled him horizontal once more and got the smog out of his eyes, he was almost certain he was the juiciest target on Daly Field. His eyes picked up

Buschere, a moot question in both of them. The assistant coach said, "It was a bad piece of feinting, Burritt."

The Green Hornets blunted their stingers against the Bandits' rocky wall. Once Burnett got through up the middle, and the coach asked for a repeat of the performance. The B-squad fullback hit again and was bounced back for a four-yard loss. Mercifully, Buschere spelled his supply of Hornets as the minutes dragged. Ron, sitting it out for a while, feeling the lumps, watched Brickhorn and Schaye, the big team's kickers, work out, and he was sure Sadecky was not impressed.

A few minutes later, the Hornets, arrayed for battle on their own thirty-yard line, went into punt formation, and Ron dropped back ten yards for the pass from center. The ball came toward him, along with a flood of Bandits that engulfed his blockers, and he kicked in a sort of panic and sliced the ball toward the near side line, then ducked to the side to avoid a Bandit who seemed bent on cutting his legs from under him.

"A punter," the coach said, in a brittle voice, "may be able to kick one eighty yards with nothing in front of him. He's no use at all if he runs scared. Come on, let's see if you have any guts, Burritt. And you gold-bricks," he threw at the Hornets standing by, "you've been taught something about protecting the kicker!"

The little Rabble fought off the next charge long enough for Ron to get one away that hit on the Bandits' thirty-five-yard line, but a tackle, unable or neglecting to put on the brakes, hit him with a shoulder and knocked him down. Ray Sadecky moved in and reminded the Bandit in no uncertain terms that fifteen-yard penalties were expensive. To the whole defensive unit he said, "Hold it down. Save some of that aggressiveness for the Eagles."

A few minutes later, after Burnett's running had forced the Bandits to mass their strength inside the tackles, Ron and Pittman combined to test the Bandits against wide sweeps and reverses. On one trip around, Ron found himself stripped of blockers and cut in sharply when he saw an inviting hole. Suddenly his feet were swept from under him and he went tumbling to the hard ground, landing on one shoulder. His helmet snapped loose and rolled away. He got up slowly, wondering how many bones he had broken.

Buschere said, after he was sure the halfback was all right, "The pros call that the hay hook, Burritt. It is the outstretched arm that swings at you from nowhere. You're still not pacing yourself. You almost ran over one of your blockers."

After practice, the Hornets and the Band-Aids crawled away from Daly Field, most of them wishing they had no cause to return. Miraculously, they all admitted, they had sustained only a few cuts and bruises. Ron, as he peeled off, marveled at his own durability and more than guessed that the West Point system of physical training was paying off. Mentally, he isolated himself from the other players and re-read lines of football wisdom by Ray Sadecky that had appeared in the last issue of *The Pointer*.

"Football is almost a hundred per cent game of movement, and a boy can never correctly use the fundamentals of blocking and tackling unless he can move fast and accurately. . . . We have always heard of the 'fundamentals,' but contrary to old beliefs, a lot of them need not be used by every man on the team. Some of them are not worth the practice time used up. This game is movement first, then blocking, tackling, and running—then *kicking*. . . ."

Ron smiled to himself. Hadn't he been a chronic kicker most of his young life? Hadn't he run out on certain responsibilities—and fast? There was just a possibility that he could capitalize on those past performances, written on the debit side of his ledger.

Willie Drumm, hobbling a little, his left ankle heavily taped, eased himself down beside his roommate. "What strings did you pull to get yourself on the Hornets? I'll gladly swap you the Go-Go team for the Bandits any time."

"There is no difference between six and half a dozen, Willie, believe me," Ron said. "It's hard to believe the big Rabble is pulling the punches. Even when that Benny Haag brushed past me, I was afraid of catching pneumonia. I— hold it, Willie."

Ray Sadecky's voice ran through the big room and scattered all other sounds. "I want to thank you men for the workout you gave the big team this afternoon. I want you all to feel when you're in Michie Stadium Saturday rooting for Army that you had a lot to do with how they play against B.C." As he made his way out, Ron checked the temptation to ask him how his fullback looked that afternoon, and then it seemed as if Willie read his mind.

"Lee only played for a few minutes," Cadet Drumm divulged. "He didn't seem too loose to me—he didn't run hard. Sadecky gave Jim Schaye the heaviest work. Along with Ed Brickhorn and Ben Zaganian. Zag looked awful good in there today."

"How about Joe Scott?"

"They took him to the hospital last night. He's got a sinus infection," Willie replied. "Ready to go?"

Skirting the Plain a few moments later, Willie said, "Something tells me we will have to say a lot of prayers before we meet Navy." He glanced at Ron and let a small laugh loose. "I've always wondered about that. The other guys pray too, don't they? How does the good Lord decide?"

"Most likely He studies the delinquency reports of both academies, Willie."

It hardly seemed more than an hour later when the Hell Cats blew reveille again, and the plebe's voice boomed along the corridor outside. "Two minutes to assembly, Sir. One minute—"

Breakfast, the first classes of the yearling year, then practice time again. Get into the gear of the Christians; the lions were waiting to be fed. That afternoon Ron worked as tailback and wingback against the Bandits, and with every offensive move he picked up a lot of football savvy along with the concussions. As a flanker he took the most punishment, particularly from Benny Haag and a corner linebacker named Hank Brazle. Brazle, he'd learned a couple of days ago, shared a third of a room with Jason Lee.

Buschere stacked up the Bandits on their five-yard line in a gap-eight defense and let the Green Hornets try to get through to the end zone. Russ Kirsch called his signals, changed his blocking pattern as Bandits jumped into the gaps. "Blue!" he suddenly called out, and the lines meshed. Burnett, hitting outside tackle, was straightened in his tracks, fairly lifted up, and dumped to the ground. On the next play, Kirsch faked to his fullback and pitched out to Ron, who ran two thirds the width of the field, trying to sweep the Bandits' left side. Cut off at the corner he reversed his field, shaking himself loose from tacklers by his speed alone. He got a block back on the ten, suddenly cut in, and was swarmed over on the seven and went down under nearly six hundred and fifty pounds of big Rabble bone and muscle.

He did not quit this time, not on his own. The coach and the trainer agreed that he should be allowed at least ten minutes to remember what day it was. Ron retired to the bench and got a mouthful of water. He wanted to swallow some but he wondered if he did not leak in a couple of places. Surprisingly enough, he was enjoying the ringing in his ears. He'd had the Bandits' tongues hanging out after that merry chase.

While he got his lungs filled again, he closely watched the Go-Go team drive against the Band-Aids, but he did not see Lee in the big backfield. He grinned only with his mouth when, his brain completely alert once more, he recalled that Cadet Brazle had been one of the tacklers on that last play.

When he went in to help the big defensive team perfect their technique of getting in on the kicker, he called to the big tackle, "What part of me are you after, Hank? It'll have to be all or nothing. A present for your 'wife'?"

Brazle yelled something back that was cut off in the middle by Buschere. "All right, knock it off! Come on, get going!"

Ron dropped back, took a good pass from the pivot man, and put his foot into the ball. It cleared the scrimmage line and sailed for a good forty-eight yards. Brazle shouted, as he fell away to avoid contact with the kicker, "Why those cracks, Burritt?"

He kept kicking. One out of six was blocked. The others averaged nearly forty-five yards, and Sadecky came over and huddled with Buschere, Nick Aronian, and the Go-Go backfield coach, Tuss McClary. Sid Burnett said, in the midst of the B-squad bunch, "You could kick yourself right into the big Rabble."

"And when that day comes," Ron said, "General Sedgewick will say 'giddyap' and ride off his pedestal."

CHAPTER ELEVEN

Day after day the autumn fever built up along with the big Army team. The B squad, simulating the offense and the defense of the first of the invaders of Michie Stadium, sweated and strained against the pick of the Black Knights. Writers checked in at the Thayer and kept the line to Ray Sadecky's office red hot. "Questions, Coach. They say you're weak in the kicking department, and that Lee won't start against B.C. How about those sophomores in the offensive line, and how deep are you in quarterbacks?"

The pre-game rally in Washington Hall Friday gave no indication that the corps had doubts about the outcome the next afternoon. The songs and the cheers seemed to shake the walls. Over twenty-five hundred cadets joined in the traditional tribute to the Black, Gold, and Gray.

> *Black, Gold, Gray, as sons we salute you,*
> *Ready to battle, and your honor defend,*

We love you.
At your call the corps true responds.
And we will fight to defend your name,
Our dear old Alma Mater to the end.

Ron was pacing the floor of his room an hour before lights out, testing out a pulled muscle, when Lew Sistak and Wahoo McGrath paid him a visit. "We know," Willie said, "you will be sitting out there tomorrow under your gold helmets. So clear out. I have a lot of math to tackle. It's tough when they throw a blockhead like me against it."

Sistak's squarish face split into a grin. "I just wanted to give you a tip, Ron. I've got big ears when coaches are close by. If you live during the next few weeks, they just might try you out as a secret weapon. Of course, Jim Schaye and Ed Brickhorn would have to break their legs first."

"Get out," Ron said. "Thanks for nothing." Besides the misery in his leg he had a small cut on the side of his nose, and he had jammed a thumb during the intramural league game a few hours before. He was in no laughing mood. Lew looked at Wahoo and shook his head. "He'll never last," he said dolefully, and turned and walked out.

The colorful capacity crowd in Michie Stadium rose up en masse when Ed Brickhorn kicked off to the Eagles from Boston College, and they stayed on their feet until Army tacklers finally cut the ball carrier down on his thirty-one-yard line. Ray Sadecky turned his Bandits loose, and Ron, from the cadet section in the stands, checked their numbers and ran some names through his mind. Haag, Brazle, Schizmadi, Wheelright, Lanok, and Jancowitz. How could he ever forget them?

Horan, the B.C. quarterback, felt out the Army line with a fullback shot inside tackle, and the cadets roared when big

Moroney was stopped in his tracks, tried to slide laterally, and was spilled for no gain. It was apparent a few minutes later that the Eagles had changed much of their strategy of a year ago. From the split **T**, Horan employed the basic hand-off over guard to his halfback, Gurski, and got four yards. Bent on holding the Eagles on the important third down, Army's right guard, Ivor Schizmadi, moved out to guard against the same play, but the maroon-and-gold quarterback countered by faking to his halfback and feeding the ball to Moroney, who smashed through for the first down.

The Bandits slanted in to jam Horan but were met by the Eagle linemen savagely blocking from the outside, and Horan fed the ball to his left half, Toussaint, after faking to his wingback, Gurski. The ball carrier got seven yards before Wally Minot, the Army corner linebacker, could cut him down.

With the ball a yard short of midfield, Army called a time out. Sadecky sent in Mike Gotowsky and Joe Outcault, specialists in pass defense, and made two changes in the line.

The satisfaction the Army coach had promised the B squad was warm under Ron's uniform when, a little over a minute later, Paul Jancowitz and Hank Brazle teamed up on Gurski outside tackle and dropped him for a yard loss. The corps, full-lunged, demanded that the retreat stop right there, and Horan replied by rolling out behind Moroney, his line hand-fighting the Bandits. With his flanker and left end decoying downfield, and Toussaint through the line and cutting out, he had to make a decision and fast. He pumped, saw Army's defensive corner man covering Toussaint, then fired to his left end, who had cut in from the side line. The ball, thrown hard, bounced off the receiver's shoulder and into the hands of Cadet Mike Gotowsky, who came galloping back to B.C.'s forty-two.

The corps welcomed the Go-Go unit with a thunderous

roar. The ends: Dutch Benhardt and Ted Sunderman; the tackles: Jim Stahl and Earl Young. Faye St. John and Jim Tallchief at the guard positions; Mort Kessinger at center. The big backfield: Joe Scott at right half, Cal Zorn at left half, and Jim Schaye at full. Whit Blum calling the signals.

Ron stared down at the Army bench, looking for Number 30, and then picked him up at the side line where he was talking with Ray Sadecky.

"They'll need Jase in there," a cadet said.

Ron had the feeling that many of the cadets in the big rooting section were directing their eyes his way. All right, how many of *you* have been out there day after day getting pounded like a cube steak? Do you want all my blood? He shook off the feeling of guilt when Army got to the firing line and threw his voice in with the rest of the corps.

Whit Blum looked the Eagle defense over, then called the play. He took the snap and rolled out after faking to Schaye, and Ron, well acquainted with the pass pattern, put himself in the cleated shoes of Joe Scott, who had gone out as flanker. He cut in front of the Eagle defensive back toward the side line, faked up, then curled back as if looking for a comeback pass to the outside. The B.C. defender spun in toward him, too close, and he quickly pivoted up field, leaving the Boston defender four steps behind. Blum threw to him on the dead run, but the ball bounced off his fingers. A gleeful burst of sound exploded all around Ron and took him out of Scott's shoes and back into the stands.

Joe Scott *had* caught the pass and was streaking toward the Eagle goal line. Ron turned slightly mad with joy, along with the other cadets, when Scott was forced out of bounds on Boston College's six-yard line. Whit Blum used Schaye up the middle, and the big fullback bored in for two bruising yards. The Eagles threw up an eight-man line and dug

120

their claws in deep. Again Blum slammed the ball into Schaye's stomach in close, and Army's offensive line ripped out a hole just big enough for the fullback to slip through for six points for Army. The Black Knights on the bench got up as the kicker, Travenko, trotted out, and when the extra point sailed over the crossbar, the cheers of the corps rolled out toward the Hudson.

Schaye's kickoff was high. It carried only to the Eagles' twenty, but it gave Sadecky's fast ends time to get down and turn the ball carrier in from the side lines and prevent a sneak along the tightrope to a score. A contingent of Army tacklers dragged Gurski down on the twenty-eight, and the Bandits returned to the game.

B.C.'s signal caller, Horan, began a concerted attack on Army's defensive wall, trying to pick up yardage enough to establish an air base. He worked the mousetrap off tackle and got only two, then worked the same play inside for three and a half. A sneaky reverse, with Toussaint on the business end, swept the Bandits' left flank for a first down on B.C.'s forty. Cadet Curt Hannsler was slow in getting up, and Bert Gorman came out with his first-aid kit. A cadet named Pickering took over for Hannsler, and the Maroon and Gold lost no time getting underway. Horan rolled out on the option, could find no targets, and began scrambling. Like a greased antelope he shook off tacklers that seemingly had him barreled back on his thirty-five, and with a couple of good blocks he ran to midfield before he was chased out.

The corps implored the Bandits to contain the Eagle offense when the big Rabble took time out. Outcault and Gotowsky came into the defensive backfield. The clock moving again, Horan drew in the Bandit defense with a drive inside tackle that ground out less than a yard. Ron, the air attack imminent, kept his eyes on B.C.'s Gurski.

Today he was closely watching the men in motion, the flankers. Horan had Gurski wide. He split an end. At the snap the quarterback ran back into the pocket, but through a gap in the Army line came Steve Lanok, Number 37. He split through two blockers and nailed Horan before he could run for the open, letting him chew on the ball.

It was a seven-yard loss, and the corps turned loose an Army war cry.

The Eagles, too eager, drew a five-yard penalty for an offside, and then the Bandits broke through on Horan again and sat him down on his thirty-four-yard line. The stadium was in an uproar when Army took time out. Cal Zorn, a two-twenty man on the track team, came in to team up with Dacey McCohler as twin safety, for the visitors had to punt.

Zorn picked up Moroney's low boot on one hop inside his ten and followed his blockers up to the seventeen, where they were quickly washed away by the Eagles. Ron could almost feel the impact when Zorn was mowed down. He rose with the corps and cheered the Go-Go team as it spilled onto the field. Lee was not with them.

Army, with the first score under their helmets, took their time, true to the Sadecky system. Play possession football as long as possible, for the other team cannot score if they do not have the ball. Again Ron put himself in Joe Scott's uniform, making mental notes of every move the halfback made.

Boston College gave ground stubbornly, hitting back hard, looking for a loose ball. On the third down, with three to go on his twenty-four, Whit Blum called on Schaye to get the first down up the middle. It was a straight buck calling for sheer power, and it paid off, the big fullback going up to the twenty-eight.

Ron ran the reverse with Scott on the next play and

turned the Eagles' left flank for four yards. He felt the jolts as Scott was heaved out of bounds. There was a block thrown down there, he thought, the ball carrier might have taken more advantage of.

The Army stalled, B.C. packing in its defensive depth, and Brickhorn was brought in to get the ball away. The punt carried short of thirty-five yards, but the B.C. safety man let the ball squirt out of his hands, and when a mad scramble was over, Army's Number 84, Benny Haag, was hugging the ball to his chest on his own forty-three. With three minutes to go until the half, Whit Blum lost no time turning loose the long bomb, and Dutch Benhardt, his left end, got a three-yard lead on the B.C. defender, turned and hauled the pass in, and ran the rest of the way, with the corps of cadets in the seats urging him on in a delighted frenzy. Thirteen points, and Travenko, the place kicker, trotted out to try for one more.

A cadet yelled in Ron's ear, "Maybe we won't need Jase today!"

"I don't know," he called back, his voice hoarse. "They're a tough bunch and they won't give up easy."

The bandmaster came up with appropriate sound effects as Travenko put the fourteenth point through the uprights, and the long corps yell washed out of Michie Stadium and swept out over the Plain. The Eagles had little time in which to unruffle their feathers and try to claw out seventy-six yards. Nearly thirty thousand spectators cheered the Black Knights off the field when time in the first half ran out. The Army band left the stands, formed, and flowed out onto the gridiron, playing a stirring, time-honored Army song, "The Army Goes Rolling Along."

Abstractedly enjoying the vista outside the confines of the stadium, Ron had his regrets over having been a Johnnycome-lately to varsity football; he wished he had learned to side-step tacklers in the old days instead of responsibilities. Maybe he could have realized a few minutes of glory under a gold helmet. At this moment, however, he hoped there would be cheers for Jason Lee before this game was over.

The Eagles served notice on Army three minutes into the third quarter that they would need more than two touchdowns to win. Having forced the Go-Go team to punt after a short march, B.C. began to pound Sadecky's Bandits from its twenty-eight-yard line. Moroney, Gurski, and Toussaint hammered at the defensive weaknesses spotted by the Eagle coaches in the first half and ripped out two first downs to Army's forty-nine. Horan dropped back and bulleted a pass over the line, with Haag and Lanok blitzing, but the ball was dropped. To counter the red-dogging, Horan turned loose a screen on the next play, and Gurski got through for eight big yards.

Army took a time out. Just a minute and a half later, Moroney shot through a hole quickly opened in the left side of the Bandit line and, behind rock and sock blocking, bulled his way to Army's seven before McCohler, Sadecky's safety man, pulled him down. Horan, on the next play, rolled out to his right, couldn't find a receiver, cut back in, and ran to the three. Moroney took it over on the next two smashes. The Eagles' point-after-touchdown kicker made the score 14-to-7, Army.

The game turned fierce. The Go-Go team ripped and tore and passed its way to B.C.'s eighteen, only to be set back by a holding penalty. From the thirty-three, Whit Blum picked up eight more yards, and Sadecky sent Travenko in to try for three points. The attempt spun wide, and then the Eagles screamed and started rolling from their twenty. The Bandits yielded every inch of ground stubbornly, and the

Eagles had to punt. McCohler took the ball on his thirty-nine and ran it back about six yards before he was thumped hard. The ball got away from him, and a B.C. tackle recovered.

Ron, while an Eagle was getting his wind back in his lungs, checked the Bandits coming in, looking for Lew Sistak, but the replacement at right guard was Number 68, Dave Kipp.

A strident note of alarm began to run through the racket from the corps when Horan moved B.C. over the midfield stripe and down to the cadets' thirty-four. Pass interference by Gotowsky put the ball on Army's eleven, and then Horan, driven out of the pocket and running wild, spotted a receiver deep in the end zone and fired. The Eagle end got it in his claws and hung on, and a blanket of gloom settled down over Michie Stadium. But the corps rose up and cheered when B.C., electing to try for two points, threw Toussaint inside tackle to miss by a good two yards.

Army's Go-Go unit, with eight minutes to play, launched a drive that carried to the Eagles' forty, and there Schaye became a casualty and had to limp off the field. Ron held his breath when the ovation for the fullback trailed off. Jason Lee was talking with Sadecky as he fastened his helmet strap. And then the cheers were deafening when Number 30 left the side line, four other replacements at his heels. Ron, when Whit Blum signaled for the crowd to be quiet, heard the pounding of his own heart.

The lines collided, and Blum went back to pass. His throw was hurried and it sailed outside, beyond the reaching hands of Joe Scott. The Eagle blitz on, the Army quarterback delayed and quickly handed off to Lee, who ripped in and through a hole vacated by an overeager red-dogger. The safety man for B.C. had to contain him on his twenty-six. Ron kept his eyes glued to the fullback as he was helped to his feet. He seemed all right. Blum put him in the bucking spot again; then, with admirable faking, he flipped to Ben Zaganian, working in Brickhorn's shoes, and the big Armenian slanted outside tackle for five more yards.

Army wanted to ice it here, and Blum sent Lee up the middle, where Kessinger, Tallchief, and Young wedged out a gap just big enough for him to knife through. Ron winced and felt the sweat come out on him as the B.C. linebackers piled on Lee just inside the fifteen. It was another first down. Number 30 seemed to take his time about getting up, even though he got a hand from Mort Kessinger, and the roar of the corps sagged a little. It lifted high again when the fullback moved into the huddle.

Blum faked and rolled out, hit Dutch Benhardt just inside the six-yard line, and Michie Stadium began to rock. But Ron had seen the block a giant Eagle tackle had thrown on Jason Lee. Army called time out, and Number 30, after a few words with Whit Blum, made his way toward the Black Knights' bench. Ron was certain the big fullback was in pain. The cheers thinned down as Sadecky met Lee on the side line, and Ron hoped he was wrong in thinking that the fullback was giving the coach a questionable cadet "All right."

Schaye came back in and hit B.C. with a handoff in close and churned his way to the two. Fully alive again, the corps yelled for the touchdown. Whit Blum looked over the eight-man Eagle line, took the ball from under Kessinger, and sneaked. The B.C. wall held for a few breathless seconds, then bent in the middle. Suddenly it snapped, and the Army quarterback fell over the line and was immediately buried under nearly a ton of players, friend and foe.

With Army in front, 21-to-13, the Bandits used up nearly

three minutes, forcing B.C. to go exactly nowhere, and the cadets' Go-Go team ran out the rest of the time on the clock after taking a punt on their thirty-one. The spectators swarmed down the aisles along with the howling corps of cadets, and Ron wondered just how sweet this victory would turn out to be. How long could Lee stand the pounding that lay ahead? From Virginia, Duke, Rutgers, Notre Dame, Pittsburgh, Tennessee, Utah, Colgate, and *Navy?* How observant had the crew in the TV booth been? And the writers in the press box?

He found himself shoulder to shoulder with Willie Drumm. "What do you think?" Willie asked.

"As if I had to ask what about," Ron said, his vocal cords still raspy. "Let's talk about anything else."

CHAPTER TWELVE

That night, after a hop in Cullum Hall, Ron and a second classman, Herb Uhler, who was a third-string halfback, saw their dates back to the Hotel Thayer. Returning to the barracks, Ron knew he had not been a scintillating personality, as far as his drag was concerned. Under those exactly 340 lights in Cullum—"How many lights in Cullum Hall, Mister?"—his thoughts had been centered on those hours of rugged practice still ahead, and the consequences he could expect if certain fears were realized. At the hop he had been unable to get in a word with the cadet captain, Jason Lee.

"How did he seem to you after the game?" he asked Uhler.

"Sadecky covered him good and only gave the writers a word or two with him. But when I went into the trainer's room to get a leg in the whirlpool, Bert Gorman was not the happiest of men."

On Monday, Ron read the opinions of the armchair quarterbacks. One New York writer had not been overly impressed with Army's initial showing. Their kicking game was below par and their defense no better than last year. "Whit Blum, the West Point quarterback, proved capable of filling the shoes vacated by Orv Richler. Ray Sadecky used his key power back, Lee, sparingly—only about three minutes, to be exact," the expert wrote. "If injuries should sideline the big fullback, Army's chances for a winning season will be doubtful. Army's potential should be clearer after the game with Duke."

After his first class the next morning, Ron met Joe Scott and Mort Kessinger on his way to the library, and the two big Rabble players seemed less than friendly. The big center slowed his step and said, "Burritt, why weren't you picked for the Band-Aids?"

"I'm sorry you were disappointed," the yearling said, and continued on his way.

That afternoon, as he ran and kicked against the Bandits, he began to wonder if the defensive unit had stepped up their violence against him. On one occasion Buschere set up a situation where the Hornets were on the Bandits' ten-yard line, and his orders to Russ Kirsch, the B-squad quarterback, were to try a scoring pass. The fullback, Sid Burnett, faked into the line to draw the backers-up to that sector. Ron, the wingback, got a flying start to the side lines to take Kirsch's pass, but a Bandit, Paul Jancowitz, picked it out of his hands and gave him a hip that sent him flying. Buschere only warned the linebacker against pass interference.

As the hot fall afternoon dragged on, wringing the vital sap out of him, Ron tumbled to the fact that he had been learning fast. His high knee action, cuts, twists, side-steps, and changes of pace were beginning to put some respect in the eyes of Sadecky's ace operators. Once he conned Benny Haag, leading him with one leg and then crossing the other over, coming off with the lead leg as Benny went in on him and got nothing but a handful of air.

The Green Hornets were Virginia Cavaliers this afternoon, and they used Cavalier plays against the defensive unit, some from the single wing, a formation that supplied bucking power and specialized in strong off-tackle and inside-tackle smashes to the strong side. It was also a good quick-kicking formation. Against the single wing, the Bandits sent their ends crashing to the outside, containing the Green Hornet's fast backs. They worked against the inside tackle and guard traps, the short-side end run, and deep reverses until the Hornets' wings and stingers were dragging on the ground.

During a respite, Ron watched Sadecky's punters work out—Brickhorn, Schaye, Scott, and Zaganian—and he felt that he could outkick any of them if he could rid himself of a mental block: if he could learn to drop back and boot without fear of the line of giants charging in on him like a herd of buffalo. He was like a golfer who could put a chip shot on the green with great accuracy if the sandtraps guarding it were removed. Just before the afternoon's trials ended, he picked up a football and kicked it nearly sixty yards, helped by a slight wind.

"Sadecky wasn't even looking, Ron," Willie Drumm said. "Well, you've got over two more years to show him."

Ron's mouth stretched wide. Jogging off Daly Field, he promised himself no more than two more weeks of this penance. The new image he had enjoyed for a short time was fast being erased in the dirt of this proving ground. He was dog tired of Buschere's criticisms, the dearth of compliments. Playing in the intramurals, Ron was doubling in brass. Did the Army expect a man to perform both the duties of a private and a second lieutenant when he graduated?

On Saturday afternoon, Ron shouted with the corps as Sadecky's Go-Go unit rolled to two touchdowns in the first quarter, while the Bandits refused to let the Cavaliers get beyond Army's forty-seven-yard line. Watching the defense stymie the visitors' single-wing attacks gave him not the slightest feeling of participation in big Rabble football. Like all the plebes here, he was just a spectator. One day, maybe, he thought with a grin, he'd wear a chrysanthemum.

Sadecky had used Jason Lee about five minutes thus far, the big fullback having plunged over for the first touchdown, and Schaye, Scott, and Brickhorn were now employed in the offensive unit, along with Whit Blum. Army was on the move on Virginia's forty-two, steadily picking up yardage along the ground. Blum took to the air inside the forty and hit Ted Sunderman with a short pass over the line for another first down. Two plays later he connected with Joe Scott on the Cavalier ten, and the wingback, after being swept out of bounds by three tacklers, stayed down. A break came into the corps long cheer when Scott was escorted to the bench.

Herb Uhler went in for Scott, and then Schaye cross-bucked to the Cavaliers' one-yard marker. On the next play, Blum sneaked in for the third cadet touchdown. It looked like a romp for the big Rabble when they kicked off once more with a twenty-one-point lead, but Virginia's scatback, Erskine, lifted the crowd out of the seats with an eighty-six-yard scoring runback. The Cavaliers added the point. Less than two minutes before the half, lightning struck again. Sadecky's safety, McCohler, fumbled the Virginia kickoff, and the Cavaliers recovered on Army's twenty-six.

The West Point cheering section pleaded with the Bandits as the defensive unit ran out. Virginia's quarterback, Smetana, lost no time getting his team out of the huddle. The clock was fighting him, too. The Bandits looked for the pass, but Smetana faked and pitched out to his speedster, Erskine. Blockers working in front of him, the ball carrier drove to Army's twenty and was pushed out of bounds. A Cavalier ran out from the visitors' bench forty seconds later, after Smetana failed with two scoring passes. The corps demanded that the Bandits clobber the try for three points.

The Cavalier pass from center was perfect, the ball quickly placed down. The orange and blue kicker put his toe into the ball, and it sailed free of the line and split the uprights for the tenth point for Virginia. Army, 21: Virginia, 10. Sadecky will need Lee in there again, Ron thought, as the teams left the field a few seconds later.

Midway through the third quarter that afternoon, with Army on the Cavaliers' forty-five, Sadecky replaced Schaye and Scott with Jason Lee and Carl Zorn, and the corps welcomed Number 30 with a mighty roar. Whit Blum went outside with the fast Zorn, and the halfback swung Virginia's left end for four yards. His ends split, a man in motion, he dropped back a couple of steps, delayed, then fed the ball to Lee as eager Cavaliers blitzed. Number 30 burst through a vacated spot in the enemy line and drove for a first down on Virginia's thirty-one. Ron kept his eyes on the fullback as he walked into the huddle. He hoped Blum would open up here. But the quarterback used the big gun again, and Lee exploded off tackle to the Cavaliers' twenty-four. Here Jim Stahl, the captain named for this game, called time out.

The Go-Go team took on a little water while Faye St. John came back in at left guard. Ron kept his eyes on Lee, who was in a conference with Whit Blum and Mort Kessinger.

The Army swung out of the huddle and set up a modified pass formation. Blum faded back quickly, just managing to get the ball away to Dutch Benhardt, who had run into the end zone. Ron missed the end's great leaping catch. He had seen two Cavaliers throw a block on Number 30 that had jarred his own teeth. Lee, however, seemed to have taken the lump in stride as he trotted off. Sadecky and Buschere met him at the side line and he gave them a shake of his head.

Fumble-itis hit the cadets early in the fourth quarter and cost them another touchdown. The score was Army, 28: Virginia, 17 when Lee came back in at fullback, the Go-Go team working on the visitors' forty-eight. Joe Scott got three on a reverse, and then Blum tried a screen that the Cavaliers smelled out and stopped for no gain. With the all-important third down coming up, the quarterback called the play action pass and handed off to Number 30. Ron saw Lee suddenly stop as if shot even before tacklers got in on him, and one of his blockers was slammed back into his face.

Ron wished he had a pair of field glasses while Number 30 was helped to his feet; then he would know for sure if he had seen pain on the fullback's face. Above the comparative quiet that came over Michie Stadium, he heard a cadet behind him say dolefully, "Oh, our aching back." If the guy isn't in pain, Ron told himself, as Lee went off with Bert Gorman, he should join the dramatic club.

When the cheers of the corps tapered off, Willie Drumm leaned close to Ron.

"They can't keep him on the bench next week down at Durham. We'll need everybody against Duke."

"Throw away the crying towel," Ron growled under his breath.

Army scored again on a long pass play, Blum to Dutch Benhardt, a minute before the gun sounded, and took a 35-to-17 win to the showers. That night the word reached the room Ron shared with Willie Drumm and Jud Pittman that an old shoulder injury had returned to haunt Joe Scott and that Herb Uhler had a torn ligament in his left knee. The diagnosis and prognosis regarding Jason Lee was apparently top secret at West Point.

Outside the cadet chapel the next morning, Ron and Willie overtook Lew Sistak and asked for the real poop, swearing upon their honor never to let it go beyond the spot they stood on.

"He's hurting," Lew said tersely, "but he'll keep playing if it kills him. It'll come out in the open soon; it's got to. Those writers are no fools."

Ron did not relish the look in the substitute guard's eyes. It seemed to tell him that many of the cadets and the members of the big Army team would remember where the blame belonged if the season turned sour. It made him think of the old cadet chapel that had been removed stone by stone and placed in the West Point cemetery. There was a tablet saying *Major General——Born 1740*. The name was obliterated, gouged out of the wood in a deep groove. The tablet of Benedict Arnold. Ron stared back at Lew and asked drily, "Is there a way I can transfer to Annapolis?"

By the time they were halfway to the barracks, he had about made up his mind to work out against the big Rabble just one more week, and the following Friday, when the Army team left for Durham, North Carolina, to play strong Duke, he nursed a sore shoulder and told Willie

Drumm that if the Bandits wanted to toss him around again they would have to climb into the stands to do it.

"You'll only make it worse for yourself," Willie said. "And have you forgotten what Sadecky said about a blister rising where you least expected it? He doesn't miss a thing out there in practice. What I mean——"

"I know, Willie. I could get to play against Navy—and a year after I graduate I will be a three-star general. You'd better hide your goof balls."

They watched Duke beat Army—in front of the TV in the Second and Third Class Club—with a touchdown in the last four minutes of play, 20 to 16. Ron figured Jason Lee had played about eighteen minutes, but while he had been in there he had averaged almost six yards per carry and had set up Army's second touchdown. It was halfway through the fourth period when he walked, not ran, off the field. On the side line he scorned the bench and kept walking around. His every move seemed to speak of frustration.

"How long can a guy play on his nerve?" a third classman asked no one in particular. "Rutgers scouts are in that crowd, along with smart football writers. They'll press Sadecky hard in the dressing room. When Jase walked off he was hitting a brace like a frightened plebe."

"And Joe Scott," another cadet said dismally, as he turned off the set. "He never left the bench after the first quarter."

Willie picked up a magazine from a table and slammed it down. "That last punt of Brickhorn's set up the score for Duke. It didn't travel thirty yards."

"You ever drop back with a football," Ron asked irritably, "and try to boot it where you want it to go with a bunch of big bruisers crashing in at you? He got rushed but good."

"You alibiing for Brickhorn or yourself, Burritt?" another third classman threw from across the room.

That evening in the big mess hall, the plebes, despite the fact that they were "at ease" and the first classmen had accompanied the Army team to Durham, carefully minded their manners. Most of them, Ron knew, were looking beyond the Rutgers game to the trip to South Bend, which would include the entire corps of cadets. The talk at his table shied away from the game with Notre Dame, already tabbed by the experts as the possible Number One team in the country.

At chapel the next morning, Ron took stock of himself and emerged less dispirited. He and Willie joined a group of yearlings that included Leo Ralston and Paul Ead. Cadet Ead sought sympathetic ears, as far as his academic standing was concerned. He was in the "goat" section of his class. "I wouldn't worry, Paul," Leo said. "General George Custer was the goat in the class of eighteen sixty-one. General Patton was "found" and had to graduate in nineteen nine instead of 'eight. After all, you don't throw books at an opposing army."

"I gave one instructor a good excuse," Cadet Ead said with a grin. " 'My senses have been a little dulled, Sir, against the Go-Go team.' Of course he didn't buy it."

The papers up from New York on Monday let at least part of the cat out of the bag. A headline in the sports section said: "INJURIES SPIKE ARMY'S BIG GUNS." Smaller type summed up Ray Sadecky's woes and prophesied a rout by Notre Dame if Army's key backs, Lee and Scott, could not rid themselves of miseries. One paragraph particularly criticized West Point's kicking game, a department that had always been emphasized by the Army coach. "Brickhorn and Schaye, who have been doing most of Army's punting, have averaged little more than thirty-six yards with their toes. The defeat by Duke could be blamed on that glaring offensive weakness. An upset by Rutgers at Michie Stadium next Saturday might well be in the offing."

"I'm surprised they didn't explain how Jase got the backache," Ron observed. "It would make very interesting reading."

"The molehill is at your feet," Willie Drumm said. "The mountain is in your head."

There would be no gloating down at Annapolis, Ron knew, for Navy would derive little satisfaction from winning over a weakened opponent. During the next three days he hammered at the Bandits with the B squad. He carried on line smashes, ran the pass patterns, blocked, and kicked. Ruffled by last Saturday's defeat, the Bandit and Go-Go units had little respect for the little Rabble's feelings, either mentally or physically. The defensive line, in subtle ways, made it plain to Ron just what was in their minds. Afterward he spent a good twenty minutes on the rubbing table back in the gym.

Army's sports information office sent the news down to New York the next day. Lee and Scott would not play against Rutgers but should be ready for the Fighting Irish. And Pete Travenko, the field-goal specialist, would be lost to the Army for at least three weeks following an operation for a ruptured appendix.

CHAPTER THIRTEEN

Army's luck got worse. Bert Gorman pronounced half-back Herb Uhler unfit for full duty for at least three weeks, just before Rutgers came up from New Brunswick, and when the Go-Go team faced the Scarlet defensive unit in the Stadium, Sadecky had Jim Schaye at fullback and Cal Zorn and Ben Zaganian at the halfback spots. They failed to get a first down on their thirty, and Schaye dropped back to punt. His kick was high and carried just over midfield, where a Rutgers safety called for a fair catch. The Bandits held the visitors' attack to six yards on three tries, and then a Rutgers booter boomed the ball out on the cadets' nine-yard line.

Whit Blum tried to move Army out of the precarious field position with two quick opening plays that got but five yards, and Schaye dropped back just inside the end zone and got the ball away. A Rutgers back scampered back with it for seventeen yards before he was flattened, and the Bandits came in to defend on Army's twenty-four-yard line. Ron, feeling forever engulfed in the big cadet cheering section, saw by Sadecky's pantomime that the coach was deeply disturbed. The kicking duel had put Army's back to the wall.

The Scarlet, featuring a pair of powerful backs, slammed for a first down to the Army's thirteen, but a flag was thrown down on the last play; the visitors had been spotted offside. The corps came up with a great roar of encouragement, and a few moments later Jancowitz and Wheelright broke through on Turneau, the Scarlet quarterback, and spilled him on the thirty-one. Rutgers put the cadets in a hole again with a punt that bounced out on Army's twelve.

The cadets failed to get beyond their thirty-seven-yard line until the quarter was about run out, and then Whit Blum, after directing a bruising drive to midfield, hit Dutch Benhardt with a long pass on Rutgers's eight. From there, Schaye and Zaganian scored in three blasts at the Rutgers line. Throwing both hands toward the skies, Ron winced at a sudden pain in his shoulder. Bringing his left arm down, he explored the area with fingers that dug deep. It did not feel sore to the touch. Too bad, he thought, enjoying a wistful smile. It could have been his "out."

The afternoon was one of near panic for the cadets and their supporters in the stadium. Rutgers tied the score in the second quarter, after an Army fumble, and went ahead 13 to 7 in the third quarter with a drive helped by two successive fifteen-yard Army penalties. With eight minutes left to play, Whit Blum had to pull the game out of the fire with a desperate long heave to Ted Sunderman, his right end, and the cause was nearly lost in the dying moments when the Rutgers defense got in on Brickhorn and blocked his punt on the Army thirty-four. The Bandits finally brought

a great sigh of relief from the crowd when their Mike Gotowsky intercepted a last-ditch Turneau pass.

There was no great joy in cadet hearts as the corps
swarmed out of the seats. It could very well be murder at
Notre Dame. Ron and Willie Drumm went over to the
Boodler's, found it already crowded, and tried to drown out
the thought of next Saturday with milkshakes. Ron kept
hunching his left shoulder, looking for that little stab of
pain, and was almost sorry when it could not be felt. Sadecky would have the big Rabble under the lash next week.

The plebes had a miserable meal that night, and Ron
sensed that the commandant at his table deeply regretted
that Cadet Burritt had become a yearling. Halfway through
the meal, the adjutant on the balcony announced that Southern California was leading Navy 14 to 6 at the end of three
quarters. There were no cheers.

"I read in a book a little while ago," a first classman di-
rectly across the table from Ron said, "about a cadet who
was quilled for taking a punch at an Army mule after a
football game. He sent in a B-ache to the Tac officer. 'First,
the report is correct. Second, the mule took a nip at me first.
Third, the offense was intentional.'"

The anecdote brought no audible laughter, and none was
expected; it had been for Ron's benefit alone, one way of
reminding him of his status in this particular corner of
Washington Hall. Quietly he requested the plebe in charge
of the "cow" to refill his glass. He raised it in a kind of
salute. "Touché," he said.

A little over a week ago he had written home about his
old plebe sin, and the return letter suggested that being held
responsible for something might be the best thing that ever
happened to him, even though the circumstances seemed
ridiculous. How could winning or losing a football game
against Navy have any bearing on the future of West Point?

On Tuesday afternoon the Army A squad, after watching films of Notre Dame football and going through an extensive blackboard drill, went out to Daly Field to begin three tough days of preparation for the Irish. Fifteen minutes after the workout began, Ron, the man in motion to the right, came in and tried to block out Curt Hannsler when Russ Kirsch threw a wide sweep at the defense. "We won't be able to run inside much on Notre Dame," Sadecky had said in the gym. "Their tackles each weigh over two hundred and forty pounds." Two Bandits hit Ron, and he went down feeling a sliver of pain in his shoulder. Don't get up, he told himself, this is your way out. He lifted himself to a sitting position and lifted the pain in his eyes toward Buschere.

"The left shoulder," Ron said, when Bert Gorman moved in. Ray Sadecky was just a few steps behind him. "It's been bothering me for about a week."

The trainer said, "See if you can swing your arm around, Burritt."

The effort put an oily shine of sweat on his face. Suddenly Ray Sadecky said, "There's always the possibility of a slight separation, Bert. I want him taken to the hospital for X-rays to make sure. He's reporting to the A squad tomorrow afternoon."

For a few seconds Sadecky's words failed to register, for Ron had been about to tell them all he'd had enough: he was quitting, and they could make the most of it. His mouth suddenly snapped open. "Coach, did you—say——?"

"There's nothing wrong with your ears, is there, Burritt?" Buschere asked, grinning. "Or your big right foot?"

A few minutes later, with a blanket around him, the yearling got into a car outside the entrance to the field, not quite convinced he was not still lying on the turf, knocked cold and having a mild nightmare. There was only a small ache left in his shoulder when he arrived at the cadet hospital, and twenty minutes later, the doctor, a major, said he had suffered no serious injury. A day or two away from violent contact was all he needed, along with a few pills in case he had trouble sleeping.

Once in his room, he felt a touch of panic along with a pleasant sense of greater importance. He, Third Classman Ronald Ellis Burritt, was on the big Rabble! At South Bend he would wear the golden helmet with the black stripe splitting it down the middle, and he would sit on the bench along with Black Knights like Jase Lee, Jim Schaye, Ed Brickhorn, Ben Zaganian, and the rest. What had become of the kid who never had the guts to make a high school team? What happened to a guy's body chemistry in the West Point lab?

He washed down a couple of the pills with a glass of water and stretched out on his bed. Most likely when he woke up he would be out there looking down the throats of the Bandits as usual. But only a few minutes later, it seemed, Willie Drumm and Jud Pittman were shaking him and telling him he had only a half hour to get ready for mess.

"Congratulations," Willie said, pumping his hand. "We all knew you had it in you. They just had to dig down deep to drag it out."

"Willie, I'm scared to death."

"Oh, you're no different than you were yesterday, as far as the Tacs are concerned. One was in here ten minutes ago, when we arrived. Look at the skin sheet tommorrow. Your bed blanket was on the floor, and your shoes were left near the study table."

Outside, a plebe began calling off the minutes, and Ron hurried to get himself organized.

He moved from class to class the next day in a kind of waking dream, the hands of the clocks everywhere seeming

142

to race toward four o'clock. And then it was that time, and he was part of the A squad, getting into the Army A. A. practice gear.

Lew Sistak moved toward him and whacked him on the tender shoulder. "Things *have* to be worse than the writers say they are," he needled. "They're sure scraping the bottom of the barrel!"

Ron got little more than nods of welcome and a few words from the big Rabble. During the film clips of Notre Dame's action in an early game with Pitt, his nerves began to sing. The Irish looked very big and very fast, and they moved like a well-oiled machine. After a brief blackboard drill, Sadecky chased them out to Daly Field, and there he concentrated on correcting a big flaw in Army's attack. Under a hot October sun he gave the lion's share of his attention to the punter elevated to the A squad. "I want you to rush him hard!" he yelled at the Band-Aids. "You know the blocking stunts."

Ron, ready to drop back with the Go-Go team, caught the glances of two of the B squad's defensive line, Willie Drumm and Wahoo McGrath. They grinned at him, promising him some lumps.

The ball was snapped back and he took it a little high, but, with better protection than he'd had when working with the Hornets, he got the punt away for over forty yards. On the next rush, the Band-Aid guards pulled the offensive center to the right and the Go-Go left guard to the left and shot a linebacker through the middle to the kicker's foot. Ron, rattled, sliced the ball off to the right. Sadecky said patiently, "You had time to get it away, Burritt. Let's keep trying."

The Band-Aids switched their tactics when the ball was snapped back to Ron once more. They sent their right tackle inside the Go-Go team's protecting back, forcing him to

143

block in, and their right guard pulled the offensive tackle in by grabbing him over and behind the shoulders. Their right end darted inside the Go-Go team's left end and into the kicking area. Ron booted the ball clear with little to spare, but it traveled over forty-five yards.

"Watch that left foot, Burritt," Sadecky said. "You're not keeping that toe on the ground on the follow through. You've got a lot of work yet on the end-over-end punt. On a day when the turf's hard you get a lot of roll with that kick. Let's go."

For most of the afternoon Ron kicked with and without an opposing line. After he had practiced endless kickoffs, striving to get the height needed to insure a cover by the defense, Buschere gave him a rest. Sleeving sweat off his face, Ron said, grinning, "A lot of work, Coach, for a guy who'll spend most of his time on the bench."

"That's right. Ever hear of specialists like Chandler, Summerall, and Lou Groza?"

"Sure, I see what you mean, Coach. But I was really getting the hang of the wingback's——"

"We put you where you're needed most, Burritt. Even after you graduate."

Buschere swung his head around to watch the Go-Go team run through a signal drill, and Ron looked that way, too, and kept his eyes on Jason Lee. The big fullback seemed to be breaking away fast and easy.

"They say you got off on the wrong foot last year, Burritt," Buschere said. "Now you're getting a chance to use the right one. Make the most of it."

That night, as Ron sat at the training table between Cal Zorn and Steve Lanok, his reception was no warmer than he had expected. A few of the grins of greeting turned his way told him plainly that the odds on Notre Dame would not change despite his promotion by Sadecky. The team seemed loath to discuss anything pertaining to the Irish through most of the meal. Before the order to rise came from the balcony, Jase Lee said, above the hum of sound in the big hall, "We should be playing the Longhorns again. I am wearing my play-Texas girdle."

Laughter, the best cure for sagging morale, shook the A squad. "They say we have no chance to beat Notre Dame," Joe Scott said. "You all agree?"

"No-o-o-o!" came the loud denial.

Mort Kessinger, the big center, said with a grin, "Sure, we forgot we have the top man right out of *boot* camp, didn't we? Or is that Navy talk?"

"You'll have to do a lot better." Ron finally spoke up. "The little Rabble hit me harder than that."

"Good shot, Burritt," Cadet Captain Lee said. Ron was certain the compliment had not been left-handed—not that it wouldn't have been deserved.

Lew Sistak caught up with him when the cadets spilled out into Jefferson Road. "Lots of luck, knucklehead. You'll cheat the firing squad yet."

"I'm not sure that I want to, Lew. When I think of going out there for the first time, before thousands of people— I'll most likely toss the ball away and start running." He laughed. "Tell me how easy it'll be, seeing you have never been off the bench."

"That was below the belt," Lew said, and chuckled. "But you can bet most of us will get in there on Saturday. The Irish eat up all opposition."

A tremendous crowd cheered the entrance of the corps into the Notre Dame stadium, admiring the military precision of the eight companies before the cadets moved into

145

the stands. The mood of the thousands changed when the Army team swarmed toward its bench, golden helmets glistening in the afternoon sun. Traditionally the supporters of the Irish soundly booed the enemy, roared their derision, yet betrayed the warmth of a welcoming host. Ron, wearing the number 32, felt like a high school dropout in the midst of a bunch of Phi Beta Kappas, as he warmed up with the Army team. Just one of a faceless mob on a movie set.

At two o'clock, Schaye, the captain chosen for the afternoon, lost the toss of the coin, and Notre Dame's captain chose to receive. After the National Anthem, the Army starting team gathered around Sadecky, and Ron sat down between Steve Lanok and the injured Herb Uhler. Sweating out the possibility that Sadecky might have had him kicking off left his throat dry. But it was going to be Brickhorn.

Uhler said, when the teams took the field, "I guess I'm the lucky one here," but Ron knew the halfback was simply talking.

The capacity crowd rose up when Brickhorn's end-over-end kick plunked into the arms of Notre Dame's Shevesky, and it turned wild when, behind deadly efficient blocking, the fast back got clear of every cadet tackler save Dacey McCohler, who cut him down just short of midfield. The high-scoring Irish offense came out to go against Sadecky's Bandits, their All-American quarterback, Mike O'Day, leading the way. Using his two great ball carriers, Cavelli and Restig, he rocked the Army offense back to its twenty-one-yard line in three plays. The Bandits, after holding Cavelli to two yards, sensed that O'Day would throw. He faded back, let the red-dogs jump in, then fed to Cavelli, who broke through a hole left open by the Bandits' middle linebacker and plowed his way to the ten.

Army took time out. Coming to the bench, Wheelright, a left guard, gasped, "That guy's a one-man posse. He's chasing us to the hills."

Hoping their line was reinforced, the Army defensive unit dug in when the clock started moving. O'Day faked to Restig, when he rolled out, and with great protection scrambled back to the fifteen and shot a bullet to a Notre Dame end just in front of the uprights for six points. The Irish converted, and the partisan crowd sent a deafening blast out into South Bend and then settled back to enjoy what promised to be a rout of Army.

Sadecky's offensive backfield, Zorn, Schaye, Brickhorn, and Blum, tried to go from their twenty-two. Zorn lost three trying to sweep Notre Dame's right side, and Schaye just barely got the yardage back on a slant outside tackle. Army kicked on third down, but Schaye got height instead of distance, and with a brisk breeze blowing at South Bend, the Notre Dame safety man asked for the fair catch. O'Day started a drive from his forty-seven and wound it up by hitting a receiver just inside the end zone from Army's thirty-five. The roar in the stadium quickly broke off, however, when a clipping penalty was called against Notre Dame.

The Bandits struck a brace and held the Irish on the thirty-one. After a field-goal attempt glanced wide, the Army Go-Go team took over on the twenty. Again they could not move, and this time Schaye dropped back and punted to Notre Dame's safety, Siano, who ran the ball back to Army's forty. Less than four minutes later, Cavelli plunged over from the three.

At three-thirty, midway through the third quarter, trailing 21-to-0, Army found themselves stalled again on their forty-one. They asked for time. Sadecky, realizing he had to play for the breaks, reached for his bench. His eyes picked up Number 32. "Go in there, Burritt. Get that ball away—and deep!"

Ron, fastening his helmet strap, wondered if his heart would come up in his throat and suffocate him before his trembling legs took him out on the field. He was sure Jason Lee's voice had followed him from the bench. "Boom it, Burritt!"

The battle-weary offensive players seemed unaware that a change had been made or were too disgusted to have cared even if the coach had sent in a grounds keeper. Whit Blum, in the huddle, said, "All right, Burritt. Just as if we were back on Daly Field."

Army went into punt formation and Ron, fighting nerves, dropped back, making believe that the Notre Dame defense was not there. Kessinger passed it back, not too high, not too low, and with the Irish surging in Ron put his foot into the ball. There was a flash of a green jersey and a thudding sound, and then he was half knocked off his feet. There was a scramble, then the shrill blast of the referee's whistle. Suddenly he realized that the blocked kick had boomeranged, that a Notre Dame lineman had made contact with him. Ben Zaganian hit him on the rear with the flat of his hand. "All right, Burritt, I'm taking over now."

The roughing-the-kicker penalty put Army on Notre Dame's forty-four with a first down, and the corps turned loose a long cheer. Ron turned a sheepish grin Sadecky's way when he doffed his helmet. The coach did not even look his way. He was chopping at the air with both fists, telling the Go-Go team to go.

Army, reacting to the break, moved on Whit Blum's arm. The quarterback threw a screen to Zaganian, and the fast wingback skirted the Irish left flank to the thirty-four. The defense spread, Blum fed to the workhorse, Schaye, who went up the middle to the twenty-nine. On the next play, seemingly trapped back on the forty, Blum twisted loose from two tacklers, ran diagonally across the field, and threw on the run to Dutch Benhardt in the end zone. The receiver made a diving catch, rolled over, and held on to the ball.

The cadets in the stands turned loose the long corps yell. Ron was on his feet with the other reserves when Brickhorn made the score Notre Dame, 21: Army, 7.

The Bandits, their own prestige at stake, struck back hard at the next Notre Dame offense. Curt Hannsler got into the Irish backfield and cut Restig down almost before he took the pitch-out from O'Day, the ball rolling loose for grabs. Kronchuck, the defensive center, covered it with a headlong dive. The ball was put in play on the Kelly Green's nineteen, and the sonic boom from the corps shook the sky when Jason Lee and Cal Zorn came in to the Go-Go backfield.

During the next torturing two minutes, Ron ran with Lee as the fullback threw himself at the Irish line. Three yards, four, then a tremendous effort that made the first down on the five. An Irish time-out. Then Ron was feeling the punishment Jase Lee was taking as he pounded inside tackle, fighting, keeping his knees driving like pistons until he was buried from sight inches from the goal line. It was Number 30 going in for the score on the next shot, and the home crowd pushed the panic button.

Lee's face was white under its sweat when he came out, his eyes not quite concealing his pain. His head was high and his back unbent, however, when he angled toward Sadecky. All this, Ron mused dismally, because of a spiteful plebe.

Notre Dame managed a field goal with seconds to go, making the score 24 to 14 in their favor, but Army filled the visitors' dressing room, content with a moral victory. Bert Gorman passed out no crying towels. During the post-game confusion, Sadecky said to Ron, "No matter what happens, you can always say one thing, Burritt. You made fifteen yards against Notre Dame."

"Maybe I'm just here for laughs," the halfback said, showing his resentment. "Well, I can——"

"Quit, Burritt? Sure, that's the easy way," the coach said, and walked away.

CHAPTER FOURTEEN

On the train back from South Bend, it was the opinion of most of the cadets that Army might have turned in an upset over the Irish if Jason Lee had been healthy and Joe Scott and Herb Uhler in any kind of shape. Schaye was carrying the load at fullback and was beginning to show wear and tear, and before Navy there was Pittsburgh, Tennessee, Utah, and Colgate. Restless, on his way down the aisle to the water fountain, Ron was stopped by Jim Tallchief and Ivor Schizmadi. The part Cherokee Go-Go right guard said, "We didn't give you much protection on that kick, Burritt. Don't stew over it."

"Is it showing that bad?" Ron asked, deeply grateful for a friendly word.

"Keep hanging in there," Tallchief said. "You could be the boy with his finger in the dike."

"I haven't seen Jase since we got aboard," Ron said. "Any poop about how he is right now?"

"We don't ask," Schizmadi replied. "It's a secret between the coach and Bert Gorman. Read the papers Monday. The writers know everything."

Bruises taken out of the Notre Dame game began to plague the squad before it reached West Point, and when practice began once more, Gorman had to put in a requisition for more tape to hold half a dozen of the big Rabble together. After films of last year's game against Pitt and a few minutes of skull practice, the team went out to have a go at the B squad. Sadecky ordered little more than passive scrimmage, concentrating on his kicking game, the protection for his booters. Ron, near the end of the workout, wondered if one more boot would send his right leg flying along with the football. In the gym Gorman worked on the leg with his skillful fingers and his miracle rubs, as if it had been the weary arm of a twenty-five-game-winning Yankee pitcher.

Cadet Captain Lee came in, the towel wrapped around his middle not quite hiding the ridges left by the special corset he had been wearing. "You're five yards better than last week, Burritt," the fullback said. "You're not as gun-shy."

Ron grinned his thanks and slid off the table. More than anything he wanted the full respect of the big cadet. He knew now the difference between envy of an athlete and deep admiration for a man.

The days passed swiftly, and Pittsburgh came to Michie Stadium, and in the third quarter with the Army leading, 14 to 13, Ron began to give Ray Sadecky ideas. With the ball on the cadets' thirty-two, fourth down and over two yards to go, the coach sent his yearling kicker in to get the ball away. Ed Camporis, in for Kessinger at center, nearly sent the ball over Ron's head. He leaped up and hauled it in, saw no chance of kicking it, and rolled out fast to his left where Pitt tacklers were the thinnest. A block by Faye St. John got him to the scrimmage line, where he reversed his field and picked up Camporis and Jim Stahl. Running close to their tails, he ate up five more yards; then, stripped of his blockers, he got by a Pitt tackler with a stiff-arm and really began to run. With the crowd going wild, he got to Pitt's fourteen before a Blue and Gold safety man bounced him out.

The long cadet cheer made him forget the ache in his shoulder as he returned to the bench. Ben Zaganian said, just before another roar went up, welcoming Jason Lee's return to the game, "What *is* with you, Ron? You wear a voodoo charm?"

"Remind me to thank Camporis," Ron said, and jumped to his feet with the long line of reserves when Army's Number 30 squirted through Pitt's defense and scored without having a Panther lay a paw on him. Army went for two points and made it when Whit Blum hit Dutch Benhardt with a bullet pass just inside the end zone. Leading, 22 to 13, Sadecky employed ball control the rest of the way. Just before the gun, Pitt's quarterback, with nothing to lose, tried the long bomb, but it fell into the hands of a Bandit, Mike Gotowsky.

On Monday, between classes, Ron managed to get a look at the sports section of a New York paper. "Ray Sadecky, at West Point," a columnist wrote, "seems to have developed a secret weapon in a third classman named Ron Burritt. On just two occasions thus far he has been sent in to punt, but he has yet to get the ball away. He is a big gun that backfires but makes direct hits at one and the same time.

"Jason Lee, up to this season, was seventy-five per cent of the West Point offensive power; one has only to check his yardage gained over the past three years. Without the big fullback, Sadecky's chances of beating Navy look dim, and five straight defeats at the hands of the midshipmen might send him packing. With his first-string backfield riddled by injuries, Sadecky has to pick a rabbit out of the hat. It would appear that magic only will save the Army at Philadelphia come November. It is rumored that Burritt is a jackrabbit with a powerful kick.

"Army travels to Nashville Saturday to play the Vols of Tennessee."

Ron, walking to physics class with Willie Drumm, could not have felt more conspicuous if he had been wearing a bright red fireman's hat. Even a bunch of plebes, marching to class, seemed to give him an "eyes right" in passing. At the training table it was immediately evident that many of the cadets had looked over the morning papers. "What big ears you have, Burritt," Halfback Joe Scott observed with a grin. "I didn't know the coach owned a high silk hat."

"What fun the editor of that Navy mag is going to have," Whit Blum called out. " 'Bugs Bunny to the Rescue.' But you really ran against Pitt."

"Sure," Ron said, no trace of humor in his eyes. "It was either that or get killed." Right now he knew he had started working himself into this tight corner years ago. He had built his own mousetrap and had one foot caught in it. The other would have to kick himself out. He fed himself new confidence, along with the roast beef and the diced fruit, for statistics could prove that they made no bigger football players at Navy than they did at Pittsburgh. . . .

On Daly Field that afternoon, Sadecky drew Ron aside and offered criticism of the cadet's high spirals. Then he said, with a small smile, "It would seem that we are both on a spot, Burritt."

"Coach, I'll give you my best," Ron said.

"Make it a little more, Burritt. You're a West Point cadet."

At Nashville, with the temperature close to ninety, Army, leading 7 to 0 in the second quarter, had a third-down play scrambled up in its backfield and pushed back to the eight-yard line. Sadecky sent Number 32 out, and judging from the derisive roar of the crowd that hailed his appearance, Ron figured the sports columnist back in New York was well syndicated. This was Sadecky's secret weapon being polished up for Navy? The thousands figuratively screamed for the Vols to take his blood.

He fought off the first stage of jitters, helped by words of encouragement from Mort Kessinger, Ben Zaganian, and Jim Tallchief. He dropped back and reached out with his hands, got a perfect pass, and with good protection up front got a kick away that drove the hoots and catcalls of the Rebel crowd back into their throats. A long-drawn-out "Ah-h-h-h!" washed out from the stands as the high spiral drove the Vol safety man back to his forty-seven-yard line, where, with Black Knights pounding in close, he elected to call for a fair catch. The partisan crowd gave the Army booter a hand as he came off the field. Bandits on their way out to take over on defense threw kind words and grins his way, and Sadecky gave him a slap on the back. "That *was* a kick, Burritt," he said.

The Bandits forced the Vols to kick, and the Tennessee punter brought the fans up yelling by angling the ball out on Army's twelve. Ron got ready to loosen up again, but Whit Blum moved the offensive team out to the Army thirty-two in three plays, Schaye and Zaganian finding running room. A penalty of fifteen yards for unsportsmanlike con-

155

duct advanced the Army to their forty-seven, and here Sadecky replaced Zaganian with Cal Zorn. Ron wondered how long the coach would let Schaye stay in.

West Point kept moving along the ground to the Vols' thirty-five, and the home team asked for a time out. Sadecky, looking for the icing, dealt his ace. Jason Lee received a dubious sample of southern hospitality as he checked in along with Ed Brickhorn. Time in, Whit Blum faked to his fullback and faded back fast. He looked one way and threw another, and Dutch Benhardt took the ball off his right ear and scored. Brickhorn converted, and the cadets boomed out "On, Brave Old Army Team."

Twenty minutes later, the 14-to-0 score remained unchanged, the Bandits staving off every Vol offense, and the Go-Go team working ball control to the nth degree. With nine minutes to go, Army let a Tennessee punt roll to the four-yard line, certain it would go in for a touchback, and Ron got up and glanced toward Sadecky. After Schaye and Zorn got but three yards in two tries, Ron went in to kick once more and, with Tennessee putting on a desperate rush, managed to get a forty-five-yard punt away. It was run back to the West Point twenty-seven, and Ron, watching from the bench again, shook his head dubiously as the Vol quarterback picked up nearly twenty more yards with a pass right down the middle. Navy had a specialist in returning punts, and so far this year he had brought back three all the way. That midshipman, Atterlee, could easily slice the good leather off Army boots and ruin Sadecky's best-laid plans.

The Vols scored with another pass, and five minutes later Whit Blum moved the big Rabble down to the Tennessee thirty-one. Here Sadecky loaded his offensive backfield, Lee taking over at fullback. It was third down and four to go, and Number 30 smashed inside tackle for the first down.

Almost immediately it became apparent that those few yards had not been worth the price. Lee had to struggle to get to his feet, and Tallchief and Kessinger had to hold him up lest he crumple to the turf again. It was evident to all the spectators, as well as to both benches, that he was in pain.

Bert Gorman had them ease the fullback to the ground when he got out to him, and soon he called for a stretcher. From the section of the Army bench reserved for the guards, a voice said above the muffled crowd noise, "There it all goes, down the drain." Ron was sure it was Lew Sistak, and it struck him forcefully that all his own efforts to compensate for that day back in June had been wasted.

Whit Blum, from the twenty-five, tried to keep the attack going, but a suddenly dispirited forward wall failed to hold back Vol blitzers, and he had to eat the ball back on the thirty-two. Completely stalled, the Black Knights went into punt formation, and Schaye angled it out on the Vols' eleven. The game ended with Tennessee going nowhere, and the Army players leaving the bench were certain they were heading in the same direction. Sadecky posted guards outside the visitors' dressing room to keep the writers out until he saw fit to let them in, after the team had washed off and Bert Gorman got to work with rolls of fresh tape.

"He's in there," the trainer told Mort Kessinger, indicating the closed door of an adjoining room with a toss of his head. "He's ambulatory right now, but the coach has a couple of doctors looking him over. Frankly, I think Jase has had it."

"Haven't we all?" the big center asked under his breath, and slammed a wet towel against a locker.

Ron hoped he would never know a longer ride than this one back to West Point. He could almost feel the pressure of the thoughts of those around him. Sadecky's secret

157

weapon! A cap pistol to take the place of a howitzer. A kicker sure enough. He had dumped over Army's applecart. He turned to Lew Sistak, sitting beside him. "When Edgar Allen Poe was 'found' at the academy, Lew, he tried to get into the Polish army, didn't he? Have the French still got a foreign legion?"

Lew looked up from a magazine. "You're feeling sorry for *yourself* again, Ron. There *is* a way out: you could jump off the train."

"Thanks, I'll consider it."

"What did you want me to say?"

"What all the others seem to be thinking, Lew."

"Oh, knock it off," Sistak said impatiently and returned to his reading.

The new week started with a heavy rain, as if the weather-man as well as the writers sought to remind the cadets that whatever hope they had of beating Navy was further damp-ened. Sadecky had only three offensive backs left sound of limb, and two Bandits and a Go-Go lineman had brought hurts out of Tennessee. The experts gave Ron's kicking some mention, but most of their copy was confined to the loss of Jason Lee to the Army team and what the conse-quences had to be. "There is mystery in the big castle on the Hudson," one sports scribe wrote. "Even Ray Sadecky does not profess to know how the big fullback first sustained his back injury, but a certain rumor insists that it resulted from a brief scuffle in the mess hall months ago."

Ron burned as he read it. The fire in him consumed all that was left of his self-pity. The gall of these outsiders, inter-fering in a family affair! This was a snide attempt to suggest there was dissension in the Army camp. He wanted both hands in this game the rest of the way, and both feet, and

Sadecky could have all of his skin. It was still raining at practice time, and that meant that the team, after a skull session, would work out in the field house. Before they began, Number 32 approached the head coach, throwing caution to the winds.

"You need a running back, Coach, more than a kicker," he said. "Buschere taught me a lot while I worked with the B squad, and there's time for me to get what's left to know. You know what they're thinking and saying. You owe this to me."

"I admire your spirit, Burritt," the surprised Sadecky said. "Maybe next year."

"I can't wait until next year," Ron said, his own voice strange in his ears. "And neither can you, Coach."

Sadecky's eyes got a little stormy, and as quickly cleared. A grin played on his weathered face, and his eyes became curiously appraising, as if he were seeing this cadet for the first time. "We'll see, Burritt. I'll think it over."

"Thanks, Coach," Ron said. "I'm sorry if I seemed—er, brash."

"Not at all, Burritt. Aggressiveness looks good on you."

It wasn't until Wednesday that Sadecky, after striving to find the right offensive backfield combination to go against Utah, sent Ron in with the Go-Go team to work out against the Band-Aids. He worked as the man in motion again, a flanker. He ran and he blocked until his tongue was beginning to hang loose. Calling a halt, Sadecky said, "Your reverse body block is throwing you off your feet, Burritt. You hit your man with only part of what you should hit him with: shoulder, neck, and side of the head. In high school, a halfback learns where the play is going. In college he makes sure who is blocking for him. You can't count on running past your blockers, the way you did a couple of times. If you don't take advantage of your interference, you might as well throw the ball away."

"I'll learn, Coach," Ron said, "if it kills me."

He received all the attention he could handle for the rest of the afternoon, and when he peeled off his practice suit he still had but one fixation; to grab the chicken that had come home to roost, wring its neck, roast it, and eat it.

CHAPTER FIFTEEN

For the next two days, his mind possessed by football, Ron was certain his recitation marks had dropped close to 2.6. After taps he ran through West Point offensive plays, the pass patterns, his blocking assignments. Friday night he came up out of a sound sleep, kicking his right leg toward the ceiling, with his voice echoing back from the walls of the darkened room. "For Pete's sake," he heard Willie Drumm say sleepily. "Another nightmule."

Tomorrow, he was certain as he drifted back to sleep, he would meet the acid test. No coach, much less a man with the reputation of Ray Sadecky, would waste so much time on developing a halfback just to let him gather cobwebs on the bench. Or was Sadecky enough of an incurable optimist to be thinking about next year?

On the bench the next afternoon, the game with the Utes grinding along half way through the third quarter, Ron was ready to believe Sadecky was a true descendant of Polly-anna. Army, the score tied, 7 to 7, was working on a first down on its thirty-seven, and Wally Minot, Jim Schaye, Ben Zaganian, and Whit Blum were the operating backfield. A fullback counter by Schaye cracked the middle of the visitors' line for four yards, and the Utes called for time out to powwow. Ron was absently staring into space when Sadecky's voice jerked him to his feet.

The coach put an arm around his shoulders. "You think you can get deep on their Number Forty-one?"

"I'll try," Ron said, and went out to take Zaganian's place. The corps's welcome to the still unknown quantity was not deafening. Ready to go, Blum leaning forward over Kessinger's broad beam, Ron saw that the Ute defensive back was playing him back about fourteen yards. The Utes seemed uncertain as they shifted. This was Sadecky's new booter, and a quick kick could be on tap here.

At the snap, Number 32 broke fast and got behind the Ute defensive man, but the visitors' line had charged fast, and Blum's arm was hit by a red-dogger. The ball was coming in short, the Ute defensive back, Number 41, ready to intercept. Ron went back in fast, circled his man, leaped and caught the ball, then pivoted and ran to Utah's thirty-nine before being forced out by a desperate safety man. From there, three short passes and a plunge from three yards out put Army in the lead. Ron, only beginning to sweat, watched Brickhorn convert. Once more it seemed that he had only been lucky.

Sadecky only let him in once more when, with six minutes left, he punted from Army's forty-two to put the Utes in a hole on their twelve-yard line. Two plays later, the big chief of the invaders' backfield lost the handle of the ball, the cadets recovering. A seven-yard gain inside tackle by

Schaye, and a Blum-to-Benhardt pass, salted the game away for West Point.

In the locker room later, Lew Sistak yelled at him, "You could pick up a chunk of tin and it would turn to pure gold. I'm only half kidding, Ron. You sure ran on that play."

"Sure, Sadecky's a magician. I'm the rabbit."

Number 32 ripped off his shoulder harness, his elbow coming in contact with a cadet wearing the stripes of a cadet captain. Jase Lee said, "I've already been side-lined, remember?" He gave Ron a grin and a slap on the rear. "You looked good. Very good."

"Thanks." He turned away abruptly and headed for the showers. . . .

The word came in just before the A squad was in their cadet uniforms. Navy had run over North Carolina, 41 to 6.

At the training table that evening, the big Rabble could not have been labeled a mutual admiration society, for Utah thus far had only won two games out of seven. Whit Blum said with a dry grin, "Well, maybe Navy doesn't know it, but we have a foot in the door."

"I really love you, too, Whit," Ron said. "Pass me a roll if you can stay in the pocket."

For once the laughter was at the expense of someone else, and Ron began to feel less of an interloper.

"He's a real gimmick coach, that Walt Eddleston of Navy," Kessinger said. "The Middies, according to the poop from down there, will wear 'Go for Five' on their helmets." He downed the rest of his milk and sighed deeply. "Well, between now and then we'll get ready for 'em. Colgate should be a breather, and then we have two weeks."

"No more than four!" Dutch Benhardt called out above Washington Hall's rumble of sound. The big team took it from there, and soon the war cry was caught up by the entire corps. The ceiling seemed to vibrate. As the demonstration tailed off, Vince Harbolik, a Bandit, shouted, "Even the mention of crabmeat makes me itch!"

Sadecky and his staff eased up somewhat during the next week, not concerned over Colgate. Every player on the A squad, particularly those making up the offensive unit, got a thorough workout. Harry Dreyer, Whit Blum's understudy, and Steve Borek, at present reasonably sound of limb, got special treatment from the coaches, for they would do most of the signal calling against the Red Raiders. Ron, running and kicking against the Band-Aids, still found certain reminders that he was not completely accepted on the big Rabble. Since the Tennessee game, however, he had no longer felt the "cheap shots" in close, so apparently they considered him worth saving.

The Thayer began filling up on Friday afternoon with football buffs, fond parents, and bevies of drags mostly interested in the hop at Cullum Hall the night of the game.

"Tomorrow," Ron told Willie Drumm, "I should find out if I'm only a psychological gambit, a wooden duck to draw the gunfire. I've got to stay in there for more than just a few plays."

"You're better than you know, Ron. Another thing, there is no one more fanatically dedicated to a cause than a convert."

"I'll think that over when I've got an hour to spare, Willie."

The packed stadium, the press, and a vast TV audience saw Army's "secret weapon" really unlimber for the first time against the Colgate Red Raiders. Inserted into the Go-Go backfield midway through the first quarter, with Army leading, 7 to 0, Number 32 took over for Ben Zaganian. It was fourth down coming up for the Black Knights, and Colgate's safety men dropped back. Ron booted from his forty-five and, with a slight breeze at his back, boomed the ball out on Colgate's four. The Bandits refused to yield a yard on two cracks at their line, and the Red Raiders could only get the ball away to their own thirty-two-yard line.

Sadecky took Ron off the bench and put him in the Go-Go backfield along with Minot, Lanok, and Dreyer, and on the second play he swept Colgate's left end and picked up fourteen yards, the last nine without benefit of blockers. After Dreyer faked to his fullback, Lanok, he picked up Ron cutting in over the middle and hit him with a pass that put Army on the visitors' four-yard line. Lanok bucked over on the next play.

Ron played nearly twenty minutes during the first half, in a sort of quiet fury. He gave the second-rate Bandit line an easy task with his long punts. He gave the Colgate line a whipping outside and had their pass defense bewildered with his fakery and speed of foot. He knew, as he left the game two minutes before the half, that no matter how much effort you put into a thing you can always manage to come up with just a little more. The corps, up and cheering, seemed to be telling him that. His golden helmet seemed to fit him now, it did not seem to roll around on his head. Sadecky and his staff seemed concerned over the state of his health for the first time when he reached the side line. As the grinning coach's arm went around him, Ron said, "I feel fine, just fine."

He went into the game late in the final period when a fumble stalled Army on its own eighteen, and he kicked the Red Raiders back into their own territory where the Bandits nailed them down. The Army ran off a few minutes later with a 34-to-0 victory, Colgate immediately forgotten and

Navy stamped indelibly on the players' minds. Ron came in for some words of praise in the locker room, but he knew that judgment of his talents would be reserved until after the crucial game in Philadelphia.

The weekend fairly flew by, and deadly serious business began in the gym and on Daly Field. Ron closely watched the films of last year's Army-Navy game and, along with the rest of the big Rabble, wished that Jase Lee and Joe Scott were fully as healthy as they were *last* November. Sadecky kept rerunning parts of the action.

"You'll see that Navy favors zone covering against passing. They play a three-deep zone, set up to guard against the long pass, gambling on yielding a minimum of yardage on the short passes. There are cracks in that kind of defense. If a zone is short and long, a fast and maneuverable receiver can get open for a fleeting instant, jumping away from the short man before he can be picked up by the deep man.

"Navy," Sadecky went on, "has that middle linebacker again this year, Carlstrom, who weighs over two hundred and fifty pounds. Our running game depends upon the way he's handled. He has wide range and is a heck of a man on pass coverage. For a man his size he moves like a big cat."

Sadecky's blackboard drill was longer than usual, making certain that the offensive linemen knew their blocking assignments on key plays as surely as they knew their own names.

"As every coach in the land knows," the coach said, "football is blocking and tackling. Everything else is secondary."

The Band-Aids, impersonating Navy's defense, scrambled against the Go-Go unit that afternoon, a second classman named Les Kyle acting as middle linebacker and wondering

166

between plays if he was eligible for a disability pension before he got his lieutenant's bar. Even though the order of the day was half-speed live tackling, the B squad was forcibly reminded of bruises not quite healed. Ron kept certain lines of newsprint in his mind as he worked out with the backs during set-up drill for coordination, ball handling, and fast starting.

"Army's rout of an under-par Colgate team and the outstanding performance of Ray Sadecky's sophomore find, Burritt, should not change the minds of the experts who give the midshipmen a ten-point spread in the upcoming classic on December 2nd. Originally developed only for punting duties, Burritt, due to a plague of injuries to the Army backfield, has been forced into the role of wingback. This observer thinks the cadet is at least a year away. Navy is packed with power in Atterlee, Fessler, Rusat, and Inari."

The practice sessions ground on. Day by day, the trees on the reservation lost their leaves and lifted skeletal branches toward the sky. Day after day it was films and chalk talks, the checking of offensive and defensive details, kickoff work, reviews of plays assignments, kicking, defense against passes and punts, signal drill, more kicking, and more offensive and defensive setups against Navy. A little ray of sunshine broke through the clouds over West Point a few days before the corps would entrain for Philadelphia. Travenko, who had recovered slowly from his operation, could be a three-point threat for Sadecky once more.

From the Hudson to the main gate, from the cadet chapel down to the museum, the signs were posted. They could be seen all the way to Highland Falls. BEAT NAVY. NO MORE THAN FOUR. It was scrawled on the blackboards in Thayer Hall, all over the big gym, everywhere.

Ron, as the zero hour steadily grew near, became fully aware of his nerves. In a few short weeks he had become a choice morsel of copy for the sports writers, a conversation piece at West Point. A hundred thousand people in the Municipal Stadium in Philadelphia would be witnesses to his rise or fall, to say nothing of the millions glued to TV sets and radios on land and sea. His old image began to nudge him, and he caught himself reaching for the way out. His shoulder *did* hurt at times. He had come out of the Colgate game with a slightly pulled thigh muscle. Facing facts squarely, he knew he was talking to himself "down the tubes."

After a tremendous rally in the mess hall the night before the trip to Philadelphia, Ron made his way to the barracks with Willie Drumm, Jud Pittman, and Lew Sistak. The songs and the cheers were still having their way with him, reminding him that all things come to those who want them hard enough.

"I feel like Exhibit A," he told the cadets. "A sleeve target for a Navy destroyer."

"Ron, you're good, believe me," Lew said. "You're very good."

Willie agreed. "If Sadecky and the other coaches didn't think so, you'd still be like me. An intramural bum. I've got a feeling we're going to fool a lot of those smart Monday-morning quarterbacks." He chuckled. "Your number is thirty-two, Ron. That's just the number of demerits I've picked up so far this year. It could mean something."

"It means you'd better not get too many more," Sistak said.

Ron's last letter from home had told him that his folks were very proud of him. The West Point system of making men had to be near perfect. His father sent a message, and he could not deny its truth, that the Burritts hadn't given the academy too much to work with at the start.

The mammoth crowd filled the stadium early. It included the top brass of three services, state and national dignitaries, and the President of the United States. Army and Navy bands played "Hail to the Chief," and the never-to-be-forgotten military precision of the massed cadets and midshipmen brought loose a reception that was heard deep in the heart of the city.

In the Army dressing room, Sadecky huddled with his quarterbacks, then offered few words to the big Rabble. "We're the underdogs and all the pressure is on Navy. It has been proven for years that respective season records go out the window on these days. I believe you can win."

Jase Lee, although he would only be a psychological distraction to Navy, suited up with the Army team, and Ron admitted to a lift in morale by the cadet captain's physical nearness. "Just give it everything," the injured fullback told him as he moved through the room.

The steadily building wash of sound seeped through the walls as Bert Gorman finished his taping. A voice from the doorway called out, "It's time," and the dressing room quickly emptied.

The bipartisan crowd greeted the Black Knights with a full-throated roar, piercing whistles, and a sprinkling of friendly boos, and Ron, running alongside Schaye and Lanok, felt butterflies in his stomach and could almost hear the thump of his heart. Almost like a mechanical man, he moved through the preliminary warm-up, trying not to look across the field where the Navy was building up steam.

When Schaye, elected captain for the Navy game, went out to meet Navy's co-captains, Rusat and DeMane, Sadecky called his starting team around him. Navy won the toss and elected to receive, and Army picked the goal to defend, the brisk December breeze in their favor.

Ron was staring up at the high crowd bank across the field, slowly chewing on a cud of gum, when Bushchere called him off the bench. "Get in the huddle, Burritt. You're going to kick off."

He put on his helmet, his fingers shaking as he fastened the strap, and on legs that threatened to buckle under him he wormed his way into the players bunched around Sadecky. "Kick away from Atterlee," the coach ordered.

The teams spread out, each man standing immobile and straight until the last strains of the "Star-Spangled Banner" faded.

Ron, the ball placed down on the Army forty, took a deep breath and checked the Navy safeties, Atterlee and Thiel. He bit down hard on his gum and raised his right hand. The referee's whistle, lifting the thousands to their feet, sent Ron in at the ball. He kicked it high and far, and Thiel caught it on the Navy five and just managed to pick up seven more yards before he was buried by a host of Army tacklers. When he came off, Number 32 realized that a lot of his fright had gone off his foot along with the ball.

Beidler, the Navy quarterback, studied the Bandits' defense for a moment. It did not shift. He faked Rusat into the line, pitched out fast to Atterlee going wide, but Sadecky's corner back, Jancowitz, came up fast to slow the fast Navy back down and let Army's safety man get to him at the scrimmage line. The corps let the Bandits hear it. Beidler got the next play unwound in a hurry. It was a slant, slightly delayed, with Rusat carrying. The Navy's guard and tackle blocked out the Army tackle, Young, and let Rusat through a gaping hole. The fullback slanted away from Sa-

170

decky's corner linebacker, cut sharply, and reversed his field, leaving two defenders off balance. He straightened out and headed for the goal line, pressed hard by Dacey McCohler. A few inches inside the line he nearly outran the safety man but was rocked out on Army's twenty-five. The Navy supporters started yelling for the touchdown.

Ron, along with the Army bench, screamed encouragement to the Bandits. When Beidler lined eager Navy up once more, then faded back, Ron yelled, "Option!" It was a hook pass that gave Navy another eight yards, and then Rusat smashed to the fourteen for a first down. Sadecky tugged viciously at the lapels of his old gabardine coat as he paced the side line. Out on the field the Bandits called time out to pick up their scattered wits, and the Army coach sent in three fresh operators, Lew Sistak among them. Navy's goat seemed to be strutting on its leash as the Middies' cheering section poured it on.

The clock was running again. Beidler pitched out to Atterlee, who was going full speed to the outside. Turned in by three Bandits, he lateraled to Inari trailing him, and the halfback swung the cadet flank for six yards before being swept out on the eight-yard line.

Backed up against the goal line, the Bandits fought tooth and nail, but Rusat, the dreadnought, finally went over from the two on third down. The Annapolis cheering section was still in high gear when the seventh point sailed over the bar for the midshipmen. The corps from up on the Hudson threw a barrage back at them. Fight, team, FIGHT!

Army ran the kickoff back fifteen yards from their eleven, and the Go-Go team left the bench. Sadecky waved Zaganian back and picked up Ron with his eyes. "All right, Burritt, get in there." He brought Whit Blum in close. "You know what to do if you can't roll."

171

Navy's defense refused to give Army more than five yards on two running plays. In the huddle, Whit Blum snapped, "Regular formation. Burritt, get it away."

The Navy defense seemed uncertain. It was third down, and Schaye was in the bucking spot. As the lines collided, Blum faked to Schaye, spun, and pitched out to Ron, and a tremendous gasp came out of the stands when the Army back booted the ball practically between the helmets of two charging Navy linemen. The safety man ran back, finally picking up the ball on a hop just as it was about to roll out on Navy's thirty-nine. Dutch Benhardt and Mort Kessinger hit him in tandem, and the corps turned wild when the ball popped out of the Navy player's hands. Faye St. John, Sadecky's big left guard, recovered.

Ron, starting off the field, suddenly put on the brakes. Only two linemen were coming in. Blum yelled at him above the racket, "You're it, Burritt."

In the huddle, Whit Blum called Ron's number. "Let's see if there's a rabbit in the hat."

Ron sucked in his breath. "I'll be there," he said in a squeaky voice.

CHAPTER SIXTEEN

Blum had Benhardt, his left end, split and Number 32 in motion when he unwound the first-down play on Navy's thirty-two. Sunderman, a "delayed" receiver, blocked at the scrimmage line, then released quickly and moved into the area vacated by a zone defender who was concentrating on the receivers who had first come into his area. He took Blum's low shot a foot from the ground on Navy's twenty-four, and the corps screamed for the Army to keep rolling.

The logical play here, as far as the football-wise spectators were concerned, was a smash into the line with Schaye carrying. In the huddle, however, Blum called, "M nine, on three."

Getting the ball from under Kessinger, he dropped back into the passing cup, his ends, Benhardt and Sunderman, speeding downfield and taking the Navy safety men deep. Flanked wide, Ron suddenly raced at top speed toward his quarterback, and with the Navy corner linebackers coming in fast on a blitz, he took the ball from Blum as Whit cocked his arm. It was the old moth-eaten Statue of Liberty, and it caught Navy flat-footed. Ron, turning on all his speed, barreled around the end and cut sharply downfield. He met no tacklers until he reached the fifteen, and here Navy's safety fought to nail him to the side line and rack him up. Ron faked in, then out, back in, and left the tackler clawing at nothing but air. The cadets in the stands came up with a mighty roar as he ran into the end zone.

Sadecky sent Travenko out to tie it up, and Ron, still refilling his lungs, stood with the long gray line and cheered the seventh point as it sailed between the uprights.

The game became deadly, and the blocking and tackling, Ron thought, as he watched the Bandits stubbornly defend against heavy backs Rusat and Inari, was certain to horrify the drags in the stands. Navy had a third down on their own thirty-one, four yards to go, and their quarterback, Beidler, passed after creating an illusion that it was a line play with Navy's line blocking hard. The fake was to Rusat, who went headlong into Army's line, but Beidler straightened and whipped the ball over the line to Fessler, who had slanted in from his flanker spot. He got the first down by an eyelash after Wally Minot came across to scuttle him.

Navy moved. With Rusat hammering at the Bandits inside and Inari running outside, they got to midfield. Here they were set back fifteen yards for offensive holding. Beidler, however, got Navy going full speed ahead again with a running pass to an end who had gotten behind Gotowsky. During an officials' time-out, Sadecky made three changes in his defensive unit, the cadet corps thunderously entreating the Bandits to dig in and hold. The ball was resting between the Army's twenty-five- and thirty-yard stripes.

Beidler signaled to the crowd for a little more quiet when he had Navy ready to bombard again. He handed the ball off to Rusat after a fake to Inari. Jancowitz, who had charged with the snap, met Inari head on, and Rusat, the middle linebacker sucked in, found a hole good for six yards. On the twenty-one, Beidler went back to pass; the Army red-doggers chased him out of the pocket and seemed to have him trapped back on the thirty, but the eely quarterback put on a whirling-dervish act that brought him to Army's fourteen before he was racked up.

The Bandits gave ground slowly to the Navy's relentless ground attack, and Ron, his whole body as tight as a drum and practically feeling the for-keeps blocking, had to admire the selection and precision of their plays. The Bandits, their backs to the well-known wall on the seven, threw up an eight-man line, but Beidler sent Inari crashing straight up the middle behind the fierce blocking of Rusat, who swept Jancowitz out of the way with a wicked shoulder block and, keeping his feet, cleared two tacklers out of Inari's way and led him to the touchdown. Navy buffs pulled out all stops, and the alien outburst seemed to lay back the ears of the Army mules.

Trailing 14 to 7 after Navy had converted, Army's offense began a drive on their twenty-seven, Ron in the backfield with Schaye, Brickhorn, and Whit Blum. On first down, the heavy Navy line stopped a slant inside tackle by Schaye for no gain, and then Blum called a play that sent Number 32 around the end, with Brickhorn leading the way, and the veteran back threw a solid block on Navy's corner defensive man, who had come up fast. Ron cut inside the block and knifed into the secondary.

The first tackler to challenge him was the middle linebacker, who cut at him from the side, and Ron lowered his shoulder, threw his free hand hard against a Navy helmet painted with letters that said, "Go for five," brought his knees up high, and ran over the man. He turned on every ounce of speed, aware of the Navy safety man coming straight in at him. The cheers of the corps lifted above the paying customers' excited roar as he hit the safety man full tilt and sent him flying. The boulder of concussion held him up for a few seconds, and he heard the sound of flying pounding feet right on his tail. Crossing midfield, he froze a smile on his lips. Run, rabbit, run. Get this one out of the hat!

Forty more yards to go. Remember, this is part payment on an old debt. *No More than Four!* Sadecky can't wait until next year, and neither can you. Run, rabbit, run. They were breathing down his neck at the thirty, and he reached for that something extra they claimed should be in every West Point cadet. A hand got a small piece of him, then fell away. He crossed the ten, the five, and then he was in the end zone, tossing the ball high into the air. Kessinger, Tallchief, Haag, and Schaye got to him first and nearly congratulated him off his feet. Gasping for breath, he tried to fend them off and get to the side lines.

The corps turned an ear-splitting whistle loose, then: "B-O-O-M! AR——MAY! Rah! Team! Team! Team!"

Ron, on the side lines, was happily pummeled again. "Yeow!" Lew Sistak shouted. "They laughed at our secret weapon, but when he went out to play—Vavoom!"

Jase Lee shook Ron's hand. "They've already forgotten me out there," the cadet captain said, and Sadecky moved in with some praise of his own and suggested the bench give Number 32 some air.

The nautical persuasion got their chance to howl again when the Navy, charging fiercely, blocked Travenko's try for point. A few minutes later, the half coming to a close, a bomb burst in Army's face. Working the risky crisscross pattern, Beidler, on his thirty-three, ran back to his twenty to give his ends time to get free far downfield. Army tacklers hit him just as he turned the ball loose, and Navy's tall and speedy end, Wahl, took the ball off his shoulder on Army's twenty-eight and ran all the way to put Navy out in front once more. Their placement kicker did not come out. Beidler gambled for two points but lost when the Army defense stopped Inari inches short of the goal line. Navy, 20: Army, 13.

The half ended with Harry Dreyer, spelling Whit Blum, sending a play up the middle for three yards, and the corps sent the big Rabble to the dressing room with a tremendous verbal pat on the back.

The trainer checked the extent of physical damage as the Army players sipped Coke through cracked ice, and soon the big room smelled like anything but the inside of a beauty parlor. Bert Gorman, working on a cut alongside Jim Tallchief's nose, yelled out, "Who's been misusing my right guard?" Sadecky joined in the burst of laughter, and when it stretched thin he called his quarterbacks into conference. Ron, sitting in his sweat, caught Jase Lee's attention and marveled at the quality of the smile on the injured fullback's face.

Sadecky, finished with his field generals, turned his attention to all. He had no criticism of Army's play thus far. He discussed the weaknesses his spotters high in the stands had detected in Navy's offense and defense.

"Their corner back, Stoneseifer, on the left side plays tight on a receiver and comes up hard on running plays. With the speed we've got at spread end and flanker back, we might get by him for a long one. He depends too much upon his safety man on that side, and if that man is taken out, we could go.

"You have found out by now that Navy is playing a reading defense and can seldom be fooled by influence blocking or sucker plays. On pass defense they are putting three men on two potential receivers in the same zone. It still becomes a one-on-one situation if you can split them. In the huddle, you have to decide who goes shallow or who goes deep and how you'll fan out."

Ron listened with only part of his faculties. Despite his play in the first half, Navy was leading, on its way to the fifth successive win over Army, and neither he nor Sadecky could gain anything by a moral victory, even if Army lost by a single point, even if they came off with a tie. All next year and perhaps the one after that Cadet Burritt would hear the accusing post-mortem, "If Army had not lost Jase Lee!"

Just before the team left the dressing room, Sadecky took him aside. "They'll kick off to us, Burritt. We want a good runback, and you'll play twin safety with McCohler. They'll most likely kick away from you, but there's a chance you can get a lateral if Dace gets hemmed in. We're using every trick today, Burritt, right out of the hat." He whacked Ron on the shoulder harness and shoved him toward the door. The bands were retiring to the stands when the Black Knights swarmed toward their bench, and the corps gave them a rousing reception. It was the long corps yell that rolled far out over that section of the city, a promise that the midshipmen had put nothing on ice.

It was soon time again. Wary, having been stabbed once by Army's "secret weapon," the Navy booter lifted the ball toward McCohler, and Ron was moving diagonally across the field as the ball settled into the safety man's arms on the Army five. The Navy-blue wave of tacklers broke up against Army's blockers, the sound of contact plainly heard far up in the seats. McCohler, cut off on the fourteen, reversed his field, and lateraled to Ron, who was cutting back from the other direction, and an ear-splitting roar came from the big crowd when Number 32, employing a dazzling change of pace along with the fancy footwork, sliced through Navy to Army's forty before he was buried under a pile of Navy tacklers.

He got up slowly, a one-sided grin under his face guard, and said to Kessinger, a two-way center, "Give that Number Seventy-one three demerits. See if he left his kneecap in my back."

Sadecky kept him in the game, and he threw a grateful smile toward the bench. Schaye, Whit Blum, and Cal Zorn took over in the offensive backfield. Navy blitzed the Army signal caller when he tried the option, and the ball went back to the thirty-six. Schaye cracked through off tackle, but Kessinger failed to contain the sailor, Carlstrom, and the gain was only two yards. Ron, on third down, took a hook pass that gained seven yards, but a flag went down, and Army went back another five because of an offside.

Blum looked over the Navy defense, then faked to Schaye, hitting straight up the middle, pivoted, and pitched out to Ron, who was on the run. Blockers working havoc ahead of him, he skirted the end and was shoved out of bounds a good two yards short of a first down. Army dropped into punt formation, and Number 32, fired up, drove the ball almost forty yards from the scrimmage line. It rolled out on Navy's twenty-nine. Leaving the field to the Bandits, Ron returned to the bench with the offense, chewing out Dutch Benhardt for committing the offside.

179

"A month ago you would never have dared say such a thing to me, rookie," the left end said, flashing a big toothy grin. "Yeah, I loused that one up, Ron."

The Bandits, most of them playing their last game for West Point, keelhauled the future admirals, Rusat and Inari, on three running plays, and with five yards still to go, Navy got rid of the ball. For the rest of the third period, the defenses of both teams refused to allow a steady advance, and the big crowd's attention was focused on Army's Number 32, who kept pinning Navy deeper and deeper into its own territory with the distance and accuracy of his punts.

Two minutes into the fourth quarter, with Army stalled on its thirty-five and forced to punt, a Navy lineman got in on Ron fast, more in desperation than in anger, and knocked him down even as the ball left the kicker's toe. The ball was advanced to the midfield stripe, where the big Rabble began working on a first down once more, and the corps screamed for the team to keep rolling. With the clock also a big factor now, Whit Blum began throwing. Rushed hard, he overthrew a side-line pass to Sunderman and on second down was chased out of the pocket and had to run, barely getting back to the scrimmage line.

In the huddle, Blum called Ron's number, and as the play unfolded, Navy, playing the zone defense, left but four men on the scrimmage line. Taking his time until he had the deep area flooded with receivers, Blum picked up Ron in the shallow zone and fired. Number 32 held on, twisted away from a Navy defensive back, but was hit hard by two tacklers and flattened out short of a first down.

Ron was in no hurry to get up. He was going to have to punt and he had to shake off the lumps he had just sustained and get the ringing sound out of his ears. Many of the spectators, Army sympathizers, booed, but Ron knew the tackles had been strictly according to the rules. "You all right?" Kessinger asked him, and he nodded.

"You guys just be sure to hold 'em tight."

He dropped back ten yards from Navy's forty-two, ran his tongue along the inside of his mouth, then spat out some blood. His tender shoulder made itself felt as he took Kessinger's perfect backward pass. His forward wall handfighting the Middies, he put his toe into the ball along with a prayer and angled it toward the coffin corner to his right. The ball hit just inside the Navy ten, and the safety man was ready to take it on the short hop with Army tacklers breathing in his face when he suddenly decided to let it roll into the end zone.

Up on their feet came over two thousand West Point cadets, as the ball took a weird bounce and trickled out on Navy's two-yard line. Ron lifted a big grin up at the mass of wildly cheering cadets as he ran toward the bench. At the side line he got an affectionate pat from Sadecky, who was yelling out at the Bandits to get the football back. The bench gave him a standing reception, but the elation in him suddenly cooled. Navy was still leading, 20 to 13.

Beidler desperately tried to move Navy out of the hole, but the Bandits fought tooth and nail and plugged a gap inside tackle Rusat thought he had made. Jancowitz came in fast to hold him to a scant two yards. Inari, on a quick opener with Rusat faking, was stopped on the five, as the corps kept chanting, "Get that ball!"

On third down, Rusat could only pick up three up the middle, and the Navy dropped a kicker back into the end zone. The Bandits charged like water buffaloes. Curt Hannsler got a piece of the ball with a flailing hand, and it was less than thirty yards out when Outcault, the safety for Army, called for a fair catch. It was now or never, Ron thought, as he went out once more with the offensive unit.

Whit Blum brought his team out of the huddle and up to the ball resting on Navy's twenty-seven. He called signals, suddenly broke them off when the racket in the stands threw them back into his mouth. He asked for a time out. The noise tapered off a little when Army got ready to hit once more, and Blum moved back at the snap, let the red-dogs come in, hesitated, and fed to Schaye on the draw, but Navy's middle linebacker was waiting and hit the fullback head on.

Whit called for a side-line pass. His protection held up well, and he looked away from Benhardt for the first fake, pumped, then turned the ball loose to Number 32, running the side-line pattern. As Whit went down under the combined weight of three Navy tacklers he groaned, but not from pain. He was certain he had thrown the ball too far.

Ron, however, had put on a burst of speed, and a foot inside the line he leaped for the ball and pulled it down. He wrenched himself loose from a high tackle, spun around and got loose when Tallchief split a pair of Navy defenders apart with a vicious block, and with the corps and the Army faithful in full cry he reversed his field and picked up interference on Navy's sixteen. It was stripped from him on the ten, but he reached the five dragging two tacklers with him. Here, Schaye took one of the two time outs left to Army.

Navy, time in again, challenged the big Rabble with a line reinforced by four fresh men, but Schaye went inside tackle as if shot from a cannon and picked up three. Blum sneaked on the next play and got just short of the goal line. Army was not to be denied. It had been four long years. Schaye, behind solid blocking, knifed over on third down,

182

and out of the stands came an earsplitting Army cheer. Tension gripped the capacity crowd. Travenko's all-important kick cleared the scrimmage line, and the corps threw all restraint and dignity skyward as the ball arced over the crossbar. Army, 20: Navy, 20.

Ron had been granted his full share and more of the kudos and the wildly affectionate pummeling accorded the offensive unit after the touchdown, but with little more than five minutes to go the stalemate seemed inevitable. For him, he knew, it was not enough. Sadecky's voice lifted him to his feet, and a few moments later he ran out to kick off for Army, remembering to kick away from Navy's Atterlee. He put all his strength, all his heart and his soul—and another prayer—into his foot and kicked the ball high and far. The late-afternoon breeze caught it and made it hang for a few breathless moments over Navy's ten, and Army tacklers were down fast. The Navy safety called for the fair catch.

The Bandits fought the clock and a Navy team bent on ball control. Too much stalling brought a five-yard penalty to the Middies, and on the next play Rusat was hit trying at Army's midsection for no gain. Beidler sent Inari out wide on third down, but the fast back was turned in and had to settle for only two yards. Fessler, punting, got the ball out to McCohler of Army on Navy's thirty-five, and guarding against a possible fumble, the cadet signaled to be left alone. Ron got up with Schaye and Brickhorn, sure of Sadecky's orders here. Get in close enough for the sharpshooter, Travenko.

"Go-o-o-o, *Rabble!*"

Out of the huddle, Whit Blum handed off to Schaye on a deceptive short side buck, and he hit Navy behind a cross charge that took out their defensive tackle and clawed out three precious yards. The Middies, still smelling the pass

183

with less than three minutes to go, loosened up their defense.

Blum called Ron's number and pitched out to the half-back. A Navy linebacker got through and hit him behind the line of scrimmage even before he started the sweep, but he stayed on his feet, gave ground for a few seconds, then broke away and reversed his field. A good block by Schaye got him to the scrimmage line and, pouring on the coal, he glimpsed a crack of daylight and sifted through, slid laterally, and quickly cross-stepped when another tackler lunged at him. Barely conscious of the bedlam in the giant stadium, he twisted, spun, and weaved his way through Navy's secondary to the sixteen-yard line before he was worried to the turf by two Navy tacklers. They grounded him hard, and the air gushed out of him. Schaye asked for Army's last time out.

Painfully Ron sucked the cool air into his lungs as Gorman looked anxiously down at him, along with Kessinger, Tallchief, and Blum. He asked where the ball was. "The twenty—just inside," the quarterback said.

Ron, as he was lifted to his feet, felt sick when a stab of pain went through his shoulder. He had to go off, and Kessinger said to him, "No Army player ever turned in a better performance, Ron. We'll take this game."

He moved slowly toward the side line, helped along by the full-pitched cheer of the corps, and as the bench playfully manhandled him again, Travenko was up and swinging his right leg at an imaginary football. There was a crowd burst again, and Ron saw Schaye pick up short yardage. Blum, with a little over a minute left, threw Schaye in on a primitive cross buck, and Army was on Navy's fifteen, with the Middies in the stands pleading with both their team and the clock.

Ron, his nerves stretched as taut as a violin string, stood

and cheered Travenko out to the firing line along with the rest of the Black Knights crowding the side line. There was a welcoming and encouraging cheer from the corps, then comparative quiet when Navy threw up its defense. Ron's legs shook under him as Brickhorn dropped to one knee to take the pass from Kessinger. He was tempted to shut his eyes. He could hear the players around him suck in their breaths when Brickhorn got the good pass from center and quickly placed it down. Travenko ran up a few steps and kicked the ball high and straight. It split the uprights with plenty to spare, and Municipal Stadium seemed to shake on its foundations. Army, 23: Navy, 20.

Number 32 reached for the man next to him and wrestled him around, oblivious to the pain it cost him. He discovered that it was Cadet Captain Jason Lee. "Burritt, you're quite a man!" the injured fullback shouted as Army players jubilantly horsed each other around. "Just as the coach figured!"

A pall of gloom blanketed the stunned Navy rooting section as Army deployed to kick off with only seconds to go. Already the thousands were beginning the count-down. Spectators were spilling out of the stands when Brickhorn put his foot into the ball, making certain it would not go to Atterlee, but the fast back hauled it in, thanks to a freakish prank of the wind and nearly turned in an anticlimax. He ran and fought his way to Army's forty-nine just as the time ran out.

The next fifteen minutes were not to become perfectly clear in Ron's mind until late the next day. Cadets moved in and lifted him above the crowd, along with Whit Blum and Captain Schaye. Down to earth again, he found himself talking into a microphone, trying to answer questions with a throat as dry as dust. Was it true that he had been unable to make his high school team? Would he agree that Ray Sadecky was something of a miracle man? How did it feel to be a sophomore who would most likely be named the most valuable player of this year's Army-Navy game?

His answer was anything but original, but it was the best he could come up with. "It feels great, but give some credit to the Bandits. It was a team effort." He excused himself and finally got into the hilarious Army dressing room, where he became fully conscious of the pain in his shoulder. He peeled off his jersey and shoulder harness, warmed by the praise bestowed upon him by the big Rabble players he had looked upon with awe only a few short weeks ago. Don't let the clock strike twelve on this Cinderella man. There are white mice running around inside my stomach, and my head still feels swelled up as big as a pumpkin. And what are Sadecky and Jase Lee grinning about over there, while they look at me?

After the shower, he sought out Bert Gorman and had him look at his shoulder. After probing with his sensitive fingers, the trainer scouted the possibility of a separation. "Most likely just a wrench, Burritt, but you've got a whole year to get over it."

Around him the post-game excitement boiled, and the sweat and steam smell thinned out in the big room. The players, the writers, Army brass from all points of the compass hardly gave him time to get into his cadet uniform. He was introduced to a three-star general who proudly shook his hand and told him he had played fullback on the 1934 Army team. "Everything here," he told Lew Sistak, "but Navy admirals."

Before he finally got away from the big stadium, he had to give the greedy writers a smattering of his prosaic background. He had to admit that a hero's role in reality was not as desirable as his dreams had led him to believe. Come what may, he assured himself, he had paid a debt.

Later that afternoon, stretched out on one of the very comfortable beds in a room at the Bellevue-Stratford, Ron let the rigors of the game drain out of him while planning the night on the town with Lew and Cal Zorn. The TV was tuned in to some rock and roll, and the phone rang twice before Sistak got up to answer it. He recognized the voice. "Sure, Coach," he said, "I'll tell him right away." He cradled the phone and grinned at the wingback. "It was Sadecky. He wants to see you in his suite. Eleven-oh-three."

"Oh, no!" Ron griped. "Not another interview."

"Go-Go." Cadet Zorn laughed. "You have to think of your public."

Ron dressed quickly and made his way to the elevators, and then he was knocking on the door of the coach's suite. When he stepped inside his eyebrows jumped. Cadet Captain Jason Lee was with Sadecky, nursing a cold soft drink. "Sit down, Burritt," the Army head coach said, a smile playing at each corner of his mouth.

Ron eased himself into a chair, and Sadecky said, "Tell him, Jase."

"You'll probably want to take a punch at me, Ron," the injured fullback said, and shifted uncomfortably in his chair. "It'll be all right. No quills involved. You know those old H-twenty-one helicopters with the two windmills? I fell getting out of one over in Germany, and I—well, that's when I really hurt my back. It wasn't from falling out of that chair."

Ron stared at the West Point first classman open-mouthed, not sure of what he had heard. When the words had registered, they stirred up a feeling of anger and resentment.

"Why? Do you know what I've gone through up at the Point?" He switched his stormy glance toward Sadecky. "You knew, too?"

The coach nodded. "No matter how it happened, we had to keep it in the family. And don't blame Jase, because it was my idea, Ron. When I first saw you work out with the B squad I told myself I had a football player, but the book on you said you did not want to believe in yourself, that it would take a lot of incentive and motivation to make you realize your own potential. So I gave you the feeling of responsibility you had to have, the sense of duty. The real story was given to the newspapers a while ago."

Ron slowly shook his head from side to side, the fast burn inside him cooling down. Finally he had to laugh.

"My grandfather used to raise horses for the Army," Sadecky said, "before cavalry gave way to armor, and he used to tell me the difference between a run-of-the-mill mount and a thoroughbred. One will shy or balk at a high jump— just quit cold. The other will clear the hurdle or break its neck trying. Well, you certainly helped put Navy over the jumps this afternoon."

"It was a dirty trick, Ron," the cadet captain said, and got out of his chair. "I really suffered along with you."

"I believe it, Jase." Ron threw the coach a big grin. "I'd give a lot to have my folks here right now. They would enjoy this immensely and would thoroughly approve."

Jokingly, the fullback asked Sadecky, "What will you use on him next year, Coach?"

"Just feed me the carrots and keep your high silk hat ready, Coach," Ron said.

He took his leave feeling much taller than when he'd entered the room, knowing now the full reason for the uncompromising and unceasing discipline at West Point. Going down in the elevator, he thought of an eighteen-year-old kid, skeptical, bewildered, and a little rebellious, getting off a bus just inside the main gate at West Point, and wondered what had become of him.

THE AUTHOR

JOE ARCHIBALD began his writing career at the age of fifteen with a prize-winning contribution to the *Boston Post*. At twelve, he had submitted and sold his first cartoon to the original *Judge* magazine. He is a graduate of the Chicago Academy of Fine Arts.

During World War I, he served on a U. S. Navy subchaser and was staff cartoonist for a service publication. After the armistice he was a police and sports reporter for Boston newspapers and then became a sports and panel cartoonist for the McClure Newspaper Syndicate in New York. Free-lancing since 1929, he has written countless stories and articles for boys on sports, aviation, and adventure. With the outbreak of World War II, Joe Archibald became a cartoonist for the American Theatre Wing and went overseas as a field director for the Red Cross.

His first book, published in 1947, won for him an enthusiastic following of young readers throughout the country, and the books he has written since then have proved his popularity with sports-minded boys.

He is a member of the National Cartoonist Society, has exhibited water colors, and is a director of amateur musical shows. He lives in Port Chester, New York, and is very active in community affairs.